George MacDonald

The cruel painter and other stories

George MacDonald

The cruel painter and other stories

ISBN/EAN: 9783744749084

Printed in Europe, USA, Canada, Australia, Japan

Cover: Foto ©Andreas Hilbeck / pixelio.de

More available books at **www.hansebooks.com**

THE CRUEL PAINTER

AND OTHER STORIES

By GEORGE MAC DONALD, LL.D

A NEW EDITION

London
CHATTO & WINDUS, PICCADILLY
1891

CONTENTS.

THE CRUEL PAINTER.

THE CRUEL PAINTER.

MONG the young men assembled at the University of Prague, in the year 159-, was one called Karl von Wolkenlicht. A somewhat careless student, he yet held a fair position in the estimation of both professors and men, because he could hardly look at a proposition without understanding it. Where such proposition, however, had to do with anything relating to the deeper insights of the nature, he was quite content that, for him, it should remain a proposition; which, however, he laid up in one of his mental cabinets, and was ready to reproduce at a moment's notice. This mental agility was more than matched by the corresponding corporeal excellence, and both aided in producing results in which his remarkable strength was equally apparent. In all games depending upon the combination of muscle and skill, he had scarce rivalry enough to keep him in practice. His strength, however, was embodied in such a softness of muscular outline, such a rare Greek-like style of beauty, and associated with such a gentleness of manner and behaviour, that, partly from the truth of the resemblance, partly from the absurdity of the contrast, he was known throughout the university by the diminutive of the feminine form of his name, and was always called Lottchen.

"I say, Lottchen," said one of his fellow-students, called Richter, across the table in a wine-cellar they were in the habit of frequenting, "do you know, Heinrich Höllenrachen here says that he saw this morning, with mortal eyes, whom do you think ?—Lilith."

" Adam's first wife ?" asked Lottchen, with an attempt at carelessness while his face flushed like a maiden's.

"None of your chaff!" said Richter. " Your face is honester than your tongue, and confesses what you cannot deny, that you would give your chance of salvation—a small one to be sure, but all you've got—for one peep at Lilith. Wouldn't you now, Lottchen ?"

" Go to the devil!" was all Lottchen's answer to his tormentor; but he turned to Heinrich, to whom the students had given the surname above mentioned, because of the enormous width of his jaws, and said with eagerness and envy, disguising them as well as he could, under the appearance of curiosity:

"You don't mean it, Heinrich? You've been taking the beggar in! Confess now."

"Not I. I saw her with my two eyes."

"Notwithstanding the different planes of their orbits," suggested Richter.

"Yes, notwithstanding the fact that I can get a parallax to any of the fixed stars in a moment, with only the breadth of my nose for the base," answered Heinrich, responding at once to the fun, and careless of the personal defect insinuated. "She was near enough for even me to see her perfectly."

"When? Where? How?" asked Lottchen.

"Two hours ago. In the churchyard of St. Stephen's. By a lucky chance. Any more little questions, my child?" answered Höllenrachen.

"What could have taken her there, who is seen nowhere?" said Richter.

"She was seated on a grave. After she left, I

went to the place; but it was a new-made grave. There was no stone up. I asked the sexton about her. He said he supposed she was the daughter of the woman buried there last Thursday week. 1 knew it was Lilith."

"Her mother dead!" said Lottchen, musingly. Then he thought with himself—"She will be going there again, then!" But he took care that this ghost-thought should wander unembodied. "But how did you know her, Heinrich? You never saw her before."

"How do you come to be over head and ears in love with her, Lottchen, and you haven't seen her at all?" interposed Richter.

"Will you or will you not go to the devil?" rejoined Lottchen, with a comic *crescendo;* to which the other replied with a laugh.

"No one could miss knowing her," said Hein-rich.

" Is she so very like, then ?"

" It is always herself, her very self."

A fresh flask of wine, turning out to be not up to the mark, brought the current of conversation against itself; not much to the dissatisfaction of Lottchen, who had already resolved to be in the churchyard of St. Stephen's at sun-down the following day, in the hope that he too might be favoured with a vision of Lilith.

This resolution he carried out. Seated in a porch of the church, not knowing in what direction to look for the apparition he hoped to see, and desirous as well of not seeming to be on the watch for one, he was gazing at the fallen rose-leaves of the sunset, withering away upon the sky; when, glancing aside by an involuntary movement, he saw a woman seated upon a new-made grave, not many yards from where he sat, with her face buried in her hands, and apparently weeping bitterly. Karl was in the shadow of the porch, and could see her perfectly, without much danger of being discovered by her; so he sat and watched her. She raised her head for a moment, and the rose-flush of the west fell over it, shining on the tears with which it was wet, and giving the whole a bloom which did not belong to it, for it was always pale, and now pale as death. It was indeed the face of Lilith, the most celebrated beauty of Prague.

Again she buried her face in her hands; and Karl sat with a strange feeling of helplessness, which grew as he sat; and the longing to help her whom he could not help, drew his heart towards her with a trembling reverence which was quite new to him. She wept on. The western roses withered slowly áway, and the clouds blended with the sky, and the stars gathered like drops of glory sinking through the vault of night, and the trees about the churchyard grew black, and Lilith almost vanished in the wide darkness. At length she lifted her head, and seeing the night around her, gave a little broken cry of dismay. The minutes had swept over her head, not through her mind, and she did not know that the dark had come.

Hearing her cry, Karl rose and approached her. She heard his footsteps, and started to her feet. Karl spoke—

"Do not be frightened," he said. "Let me see you home.   I will walk behind you."

"Who are you?" she rejoined.

"Karl Wolkenlicht."

"I have heard of you. Thank you. I can go home alone."

Yet, as if in a half-dreamy, half-unconscious mood, she accepted his offered hand to lead her through the graves, and allowed him to walk beside her, till, reaching the corner of a narrow street, she suddenly bade him good night and vanished. He thought it better not to follow her, so he returned her good night and went home.

How to see her again was his first thought the next day; as, in fact, how to see her at all had been his first thought for many days. She went nowhere that ever he heard of; she knew nobody that he knew; she was never seen at church, or at market; never seen in the street. Her home had a dreary, desolate aspect. It looked as if no one ever went out or in. It was like a place on which decay had fallen because there was no indwelling spirit. The mud of years was baked upon its door, and no faces looked out of its dusty windows.

How then could she be the most celebrated beauty of Prague? How, then, was it that Heinrich Höllenrachen knew her the moment he saw her? Above all, how was it that Karl Wolkenlicht had, in fact, fallen in love with her before ever he saw her? It was thus:

Her father was a painter. Belonging thus to the public, it had taken the liberty of re-naming him. Every one called him Teufelsbürst, or Devilsbrush. It was a name with which, to judge from the nature of his representations, he could hardly fail to be pleased. For, not as a nightmare-dream, which may alternate with the loveliest visions, but as his ordinary every-day-work, he delighted to represent human suffering.

Not an aspect of human woe or torture, as expressed in countenance or limb, came before his willing imagination, but he bore it straightway to his easel. In the moments that precede sleep, when the black space before the eyes of the poet teems with lovely faces, or dawns into a spirit-landscape, face after face of suffering, in all varieties of expression, would crowd, as if compelled by the accompanying fiends, to present themselves, in awful levée, before the inner eye of the expectant master. Then he would rise, light his lamp, and, with rapid hand, make notes of his visions; recording with swift successive sweeps of his pencil, every individual face which had rejoiced his evil fancy. Then he would return to his couch, and, well satisfied, fall asleep to dream yet further embodiments of human ill.

What wrong could man or mankind have done him, to be thus fearfully pursued by the vengeance of the artist's hate?

Another characteristic of the faces and forms which he drew was, that they were all beautiful in the original idea. The lines of each face, however distorted by pain, would have been, in rest, absolutely beautiful; and the whole of the execution bore witness to the fact that upon this original beauty the painter had directed the artillery of anguish, to bring down the sky-soaring heights of its divinity to the level of a hated existence. To do this, he worked in perfect accordance with artistic law, falsifying no line of the original forms. It was the suffering, rather than his pencil, that wrought the change. The latter was the willing instrument to record what the imagination conceived with a cruelty composed enough to be correct.

To enhance the beauty he had thus distorted, and so to enhance yet further the suffering that produced the distortion, he would often represent attendant demons, whom he made as ugly as his imagination could compass; avoiding, however, all grotesqueness beyond what was sufficient to indicate that they were demons, and not men. Their ugliness rose from hate, envy, and all evil passions; amongst which he especially delighted to represent a gloating exultation over human distress. And often in the midst of his clouds of demon faces, would some one who knew him recognise the painter's own likeness, such as the mirror might have presented it to him when he was busiest over the incarnation of some exquisite torture.

But, apparently with the wish to avoid being supposed to choose such representations for their own sakes, he always found a story, often in the histories of the church, whose name he gave to the painting, and which he pretended to have inspired the pictorial conception. No one, however, who looked upon his suffering martyrs, could suppose for a moment that he honoured their martyrdom. They were but the vehicles for his hate of humanity. He was the torturer, and not Diocletian or Nero.

But, stranger yet to tell, there was no picture, whatever its subject, into which he did not introduce one form of placid and harmonious loveliness. In this, however, his fierceness was only more fully displayed. For in no case did this form manifest any relation either to the actors or the endurers in the picture. Hence its very loveliness became almost hateful to those who beheld it. Not a shade crossed the still sky of that brow, not a ripple disturbed the still sea of that cheek. She did not hate, she did not love the sufferers: the painter would not have her hate, for that would be to the injury of her loveliness; would not have her love, for he hated. Sometimes she floated above, as a still, unobservant angel, her gaze turned upward, dreaming along, careless as a white summer cloud, across the blue. If she looked down on the scene below, it was only that the beholder might see that she saw and did not care; that not a feather of her outspread pinions would quiver at the sight. Sometimes she would stand in the crowd, as if she had been copied there from another picture, and had nothing to do with this one, nor any right to be in it at all. Or when the red blood was trickling drop by drop from the crushed limb, she might be seen standing nearest, smiling over a primrose or the bloom on a peach. Some had said that she was the painter's wife; that she had been false to him; that he had killed her; and, finding that that was no sufficing revenge, thus half in love, and half in deepest hate, immortalized his vengeance. But it was now universally understood that it was his daughter, of whose loveliness extravagant reports went abroad; though all said, doubtless reading this from her father's pictures, that she was a beauty without a heart. Strange theories of something else supplying its place were rife among the anatomical students. With the girl in the pictures, the wild imagination of Lottchen, probably in part from her apparently absolute unattainableness and her undisputed heartlessness, had fallen in love, as far as the mere imagination can fall in love.

But again, how was he to see her? He haunted the house night after night. Those blue eyes never met his. No step responsive to his came from that door. It seemed to have been so long unopened that it had grown as fixed and hard as the stones that held its bolts in their passive clasp. He dared not watch in the day-time, and with all his watching at night, he never saw father or daughter or domestic cross the threshold. Little he thought that, from a shot-window near the door, a pair of blue eyes, like Lilith's, but paler and colder, were watching him, just as a spider watches the fly that is likely ere long to fall into his toils. And into those toils Karl soon fell. For her form darkened the page; her form stood on the threshold of sleep; and when, overcome with watching, he did enter its precincts, her form entered with him, and walked by his side. He must find her; or the world might go to the bottom‑less pit for him. But how?

Yes. He would be a painter. Teufelsbürst would receive him as a humble apprentice. He would grind his colours, and Teufelsbürst would teach him the mysteries of the science which is the handmaiden of art. Then he might see *her*, and that was all his ambition.

In the clear morning light of a day in autumn, when the leaves were beginning to fall seared from the hand of that Death which has his dance in the chapels of nature as well as in the cathedral aisles of men—he walked up and knocked at the dingy door. The spider painter opened it himself. He

was a little man, meagre and pallid, with those
faded blue eyes, a low nose in three distinct
divisions, and thin, curveless, cruel lips. He
wore no hair on his face; but long grey locks,
long as a woman's, were scattered over his
shoulders, and hung down on his breast. When
Wolkenlicht had explained his errand, he smiled
a smile in which hypocrisy could not hide the
cunning, and, after many difficulties, consented
to receive him as a pupil, on condition that
he would become an inmate of his house.
Wolkenlicht's heart bounded with delight, which
he tried to hide: the second smile of Teufelsbürst might have shown him that he had ill
succeeded. The fact that he was not a native
of Prague, but, coming from a distant part of
the country, was entirely his own master in
the city, rendered this condition perfectly easy
to fulfil; and that very afternoon, he entered

the studio of Teufelsbürst as his scholar and servant.

It was a great room, filled with the appliances and results of art. Many pictures, festooned with cobwebs, were hung carelessly on the dirty walls. Others, half finished, leaned against them, on the floor. Several, in different stages of progress, stood upon easels. But all spoke the cruel bent of the artist's genius. In one corner a lay-figure was extended on a couch, covered with a pall of black velvet. Through its folds, the form beneath was easily discernible; and one hand and fore-arm protruded from beneath it, at right angles to the rest of the frame. Lottchen could not help shuddering when he saw it. Although he overcame the feeling in a moment, he felt a great repugnance to seating himself with his back towards it, as the arrangement of an easel, at which Teufelsbürst wished him to draw, rendered necessary. He contrived to edge himself round, so that when he lifted his eyes he should see the figure, and be sure that it could not rise without his being aware of it. But his master saw and understood his altered position; and under some pretence about the light, compelled him to resume the position in which he had placed him at first; after which he sat watching, over the top of his picture, the expression of his countenance as he tried to draw; reading in it the horrid fancy that the figure under the pall had risen, and was stealthily approaching to look over his shoulder. But Lottchen resisted the feeling, and, being already no contemptible draughtsman, was soon interested enough to forget it. And then, any moment, *she* might enter.

Now began a system of slow torture, for the chance of which the painter had been long on the watch—especially since he had first seen Karl lingering about the house. His opportunities of seeing physical suffering were nearly enough even for the diseased necessities of his art; but now he had one in his power, on whom, his own will fettering him, he could try any experiments he pleased for the production of a kind of suffering, in the observation of which he did not consider that he had yet had sufficient experience. He would hold the very heart of the youth in his hand, and wring it and torture it to his own content. And lest Karl should be strong enough to prevent those expressions of pain for which he lay on the watch, he would make use of further means, known to himself, and known to few besides.

All that day Karl saw nothing of Lilith; but he heard her voice once—and that was enough for one day. The next, she was sitting to her father the greater part of the day, and he could see her as often as he dared glance up from his drawing. She had looked at him when she entered, but had shown no sign of recognition; and all day long she took no further notice of him. He hoped, at first, that this came of the intelligence of love; but he soon began to doubt it. For he saw that, with the holy shadow of sorrow, all that distinguished the expression of her countenance from that which the painter so constantly reproduced, had vanished likewise. It was the very face of the unheeding angel whom, as often as he lifted his eyes higher than hers, he saw on the wall above her, playing on a psaltery in the smoke of the torment ascending for ever from burning Babylon.—The power of the painter had not merely wrought for the representation of the woman of his imagination: it had had scope as well in realizing her.

Karl soon began to see that communication,

other than of the eyes, was all but hopeless; and to any attempt in that way she seemed altogether indisposed to respond. Nor, if she had wished it, would it have been safe; for as often as he glanced towards her, instead of hers, he met the blue eyes of the painter, gleaming upon him like winter-lightning. His tones, his gestures, his words, seemed kind: his glance and his smile refused to be disguised.

The first day he dined alone in the studio, waited upon by an old woman; the next he was admitted to the family table, with Teufels-bürst and Lilith. The room offered a strange contrast to the study. As far as handicraft, directed by a sumptuous taste, could construct a house-paradise, this was one. But it seemed rather a paradise of demons; for the walls were covered with Teufelsbürst's paintings. During the dinner, Lilith's gaze scarcely met that of Wolkenlicht; and once or twice, when their eyes did meet, her glance was so perfectly unconcerned, that Karl wished he might look at her for ever without the fear of her looking at him again. She seemed like one whose love had rushed out glowing with seraphic fire, to be frozen to death in a more than wintry cold: she now walked lonely without her love. In the evenings, he was expected to continue his drawing by lamp-light; and at night he was conducted by Teufelsbürst to his chamber. Not once did he allow him to proceed thither alone, and not once did he leave him there without locking and bolting the door on the outside. But he felt nothing except the coldness of Lilith.

Day after day she sat to her father, in every variety of costume that could best show the variety of her beauty. How much greater that beauty might be, if it ever blossomed into a beauty of soul, Wolkenlicht never imagined; for he soon loved her enough to attribute to her all the possibilities of her face as actual possessions of her being. To account for everything that seemed to contradict this perfection, his brain was prolific in inventions; till he was compelled at last to see that she was in the condition of a rose-bud, which, on the point of blossoming, has been chilled into a changeless bud by the cold of an untimely frost. For one day, after the father and daughter had become a little more accustomed to his silent presence, a conversation began between them, which went on until he saw that Teufelsbürst believed in nothing except his art. How much of his feeling for that could be dignified by the name of belief, seeing its objects were such as they were, might have been questioned. It seemed to Wolkenlicht to amount only to this: that, amidst a thousand distastes, it was a pleasant thing to re-produce on the canvas the forms he beheld around him, modifying them to express the prevailing feelings of his own mind.

A more desolate communication between souls than that which then passed between father and daughter could hardly be imagined. The father spoke of humanity and all its experiences in a tone of the bitterest scorn. He despised men and himself amongst them; and rejoiced to think that the generations rose and vanished, brood after brood, as the crops of corn grew and disappeared. Lilith, who listened to it all unmoved, taking only an intellectual interest in the question, remarked that even the corn had more life than that; for, after its death, it rose again in the new crop. Whether she meant that the corn was therefore superior to man, forgetting that the superior can produce being without losing its own, or only advanced an objection to her father's argument, Wolkenlicht could not tell. But Teufelsbürst laughed like the sound of a saw, and said: "Follow out the analogy, my Lilith, and you will see that man is like the corn that springs again after it is buried; but unfortunately the only result we know of is a vampire."

Wolkenlicht looked up, and saw a shudder pass through the frame, and over the pale thin face of the painter. This he could not account for. But Teufelsbürst could have explained it, for there were strange whispers abroad, and they had reached his ear; and his philosophy was not quite enough for them. But the laugh with which Lilith met this frightful attempt at wit, grated dreadfully on Wolkenlicht's feeling. With her, too, however, a reaction seemed to follow. For, turning round a moment after, and looking at the picture on which her father was working, the tears rose in her eyes, and she said: "Oh! father, how like my mother you have made me this time!"   "Child!" retorted the painter with a cold fierceness, "you have no mother. That which is gone out is gone out. Put no name in my hearing on that which is not. Where no substance is, how can there be a name?"

Lilith rose and left the room. Wolkenlicht now understood that Lilith was a frozen bud, and could not blossom into a rose. But pure love lives by faith. It loves the vaguely beheld and unrealized ideal. It dares believe that the loved is not all that she ever seemed. It is in virtue of this that love loves on. And it was in virtue of this, that Wolkenlicht loved Lilith yet more after he discovered what a grave of misery her unbelief was digging for her within her own soul. For her sake he would bear anything—bear even with calmness the torments of his own love; he would stay on, hoping and hoping.—The text, that we know not what a day may bring forth, is just as true of good things as of evil things; and out of Time's womb the facts must come.

But with the birth of this resolution to endure, his suffering abated; his face grew more calm; his love, no less earnest, was less imperious; and he did not look up so often from his work when Lilith was present. The master could see that his pupil was more at ease, and that he was making rapid progress in his art. This did not suit his designs, and he would betake himself to his further schemes.

For this purpose he proceeded first to simulate a friendship for Wolkenlicht, the manifestations of which he gradually increased, until, after a day or two, he asked him to drink wine with him in the evening. Karl readily agreed. The painter produced some of his best; but took care not to allow Lilith to taste it; for he had cunningly prepared and mingled with it a decoction of certain herbs and other ingredients, exercising specific actions upon the brain, and tending to the inordinate excitement of those portions of it which are principally under the rule of the imagination. By the reaction of the brain during the operation of these stimulants, the imagination is filled with suggestions and images. The nature of these is determined by the prevailing mood of the time. They are such as the imagination would produce of itself; but increased in number and intensity. Teufelsbürst, without philosophizing about it, called his preparation simply a love-philtre, a concoction well known by name, but the composition of which was the secret of only a few. Wolkenlicht had, of course, not the least suspicion of the treatment to which he was subjected.

Teufelsbürst was, however, doomed to fresh

disappointment. Not that his potion failed in the anticipated effect; for now Karl's real sufferings began; but that such was the strength of Karl's will, and his fear of doing anything that might give a pretext for banishing him from the presence of Lilith, that he was able to conceal his feelings far too successfully for the satisfaction of Teufelsbürst's art. Yet he had to fetter himself with all the restraints that self-exhortation could load him with, to refrain from falling at the feet of Lilith and kissing the hem of her garment. For that, as the lowliest part of all that surrounded her, itself kissing the earth, seemed to come nearest within the reach of his ambition, and therefore to draw him the most.

No doubt the painter had experience and penetration enough to perceive that he was suffering intensely; but he wanted to see the suffering embodied in outward signs, bringing it within the region over which his pencil held sway. He kept on, therefore, trying one thing after another, and rousing the poor youth to agony; till to his other sufferings were added, at length, those of failing health; a fact which notified itself evidently enough even for Teufelsbürst, though its signs were not of the sort he chiefly desired. But Karl endured all bravely.

Meantime, for various reasons, he scarcely ever left the house.

I must now interrupt the course of my story to introduce another element.

A few years before the period of my tale, a certain shoemaker of the city had died under circumstances more than suggestive of suicide. He was buried, however, with such precautions, that six weeks elapsed before the rumour of the facts broke out; upon which rumour, not before, the most fearful reports began to be circulated, supported by what seemed to the people of Prague incontestable evidence.—A *spectrum* of the deceased appeared to multitudes of persons, playing horrible pranks, and occasioning indescribable consternation throughout the whole town. This went on till at last, about eight months after his burial, the magistrates caused his body to be dug up; when it was found in just the condition of the bodies of those who in the eastern countries of Europe are called *vampires*. They buried the corpse under the gallows; but neither the digging up nor the re-burying were of avail to banish the spectre. Again the spade and pick-axe were set to work, and the dead man being found considerably improved in *condition* since his last interment, was, with various horrible indignities, burnt to ashes, "after which the *spectrum* was never seen more."

And a second epidemic of the same nature had

broken out a little before the period to which I have brought my story.

About midnight, after a calm frosty day, for it was now winter, a terrible storm of wind and snow came on. The tempest howled frightfully about the house of the painter, and Wolkenlicht found some solace in listening to the uproar, for his troubled thoughts would not allow him to sleep. It raged on all the next three days, till about noon on the fourth day, when it suddenly fell, and all was calm. The following night, Wolkenlicht, lying awake, heard unaccountable noises in the next house, as of things thrown about, of kicking and fighting horses, and of opening and shutting gates. Flinging wide his lattice and looking out, the noise of howling dogs came to him from every quarter of the town. The moon was bright and the air was still. In a little while he heard the sounds of a horse going at full gallop round the house, so that it shook as if it would fall; and flashes of light shone into his room. How much of this may have been owing to the effect of the drugs on poor Lottchen's brain, I leave my readers to determine. But when the family met at breakfast in the morning, Teufelsbürst, who had been already out of doors, reported that he had found the marks of strange feet in the snow, all about the house and through the garden at the back; stating, as his belief, that the tracks must be continued over the roofs, for there was no passage otherwise. There was a wicked gleam in his eye as he spoke; and Lilith believed that he was only trying an experiment on Karl's nerves. He persisted that he had never seen any footprints of the sort before. Karl informed him of his experiences during the night; upon which Teufelsbürst looked a little graver still, and proceeded to tell them that the storm, whose snow was still covering the ground, had arisen the very moment that their next door neighbour died, and had ceased as suddenly the moment he was buried, though it had raved furiously all the time of the funeral, so that "it made men's bodies quake and their teeth chatter in their heads." Karl had heard that the man, whose name was John Kuntz, was dead and buried. He knew that he had been a very wealthy, and therefore most respectable, alderman of the town; that he had been very fond of horses; and that he had died in consequence of a kick received from one of his own, as he was looking at his hoof. But he had not heard that, just before he died, a black cat "opened the casement with her nails, ran to his bed, and violently scratched his face and the bolster, as if she endeavoured by force to remove him out of the place where he lay. But the cat afterwards was suddenly gone, and she was no sooner gone, but he breathed his last."

So said Teufelsbürst, as the reporter of the town-talk. Lilith looked very pale and terrified; and it was perhaps owing to this that the painter brought no more tales home with him. There were plenty to bring, but he heard them all and said nothing. The fact was that the philosopher himself could not resist the infection of the fear that was literally raging in the city; and perhaps the reports that he himself had sold himself to the devil, had sufficient response from his own evil conscience to add to the influence of the epidemic upon him. The whole place was infested with the presence of the dead Kuntz, till scarce a man or woman would dare to be alone. He strangled old men; insulted women; squeezed children to death; knocked out the brains of dogs against the ground; pulled up posts; turned milk into blood nearly killed a worthy clergyman by breathing upon him the intolerable airs of the grave, cold and malignant and noisome; and, in short, filled the city with a perfect madness of fear, so that every report was believed without the smallest doubt or investigation.

Though Teufelsbürst brought home no more of the town-talk, the old servant was a faithful purveyor, and frequented the news-mart assiduously. Indeed she had some nightmare experiences of her own that she was proud to add to the stock of horrors which the city enjoyed with such a hearty community of goods. For those regions were not far removed from the very birth-place and home of the vampire. The belief in vampires is the quintessential concentration and embodiment of all the passion of fear in Hungary and the adjacent regions. Nor of all the other inventions of the human imagination, has there ever been one so perfect in crawling terror as this. Lilith and Karl were quite familiar with the popular ideas on the subject. It did not require to be explained to them, that a vampire was a body retaining a kind of animal life after the soul had departed. If any relation continued between it and the vanished ghost, it was only sufficient to make it restless in its grave. Possessed of vitality enough to keep it uncorrupted and pliant, its only instinct was a blind hunger for the sole food which could keep its awful life persistent—living human blood. Hence it, or if not it, a sort of semi-material exhalation or essence of it, retaining its form and material relations, crept from its tomb, and went roaming about till it found some one asleep, towards whom it had an attraction, founded on old affection. It sucked the blood of this unhappy being, transferring so much of its life to itself as a vampire could assimilate. Death was the certain consequence. If suspicion conjectured aright, and they opened the proper grave, the body of the vampire would be found perfectly fresh and plump, sometimes indeed of rather florid complexion;—with grown hair, eyes half open, and the stains of recent blood about its greedy leech-like lips. Nothing remained but to consume the corpse to ashes, upon which the vampire would show itself no more. But what added infinitely to the horror was the certainty that whoever died from the mouth of the vampire, wrinkled grandsire, or delicate maiden, must in turn rise from the grave, and go forth a vampire, to suck the blood of the dearest left behind. This was the generation of the vampire brood. Lilith trembled at the very name of the creature. Karl was too much in love to be afraid of anything. Yet the evident fear of the unbelieving painter took a hold of his imagination;

and, under the influence of the potions of which he still partook unwittingly—when he was not thinking about Lilith, he was thinking about the vampire.

Meantime, the condition of things in the painter's household continued much the same for Wolkenlicht—work all day; no communication between the young people; the dinner and the wine; silent reading when work was done, with stolen glances many over the top of the book, glances that were never returned; the cold good night; the locking of the door; the wakeful night and the drowsy morning. But at length a change came, and sooner than any of the party had expected. For, whether it was that the impatience of Teufelsbürst had urged him to yet more dangerous experiments, or that the continuance of those he had been so long employing had overcome at length the vitality of Wolkenlicht—one afternoon, as he was sitting at his work, he suddenly dropped from his chair, and his master hurrying to him in some alarm, found him rigid and apparently lifeless. Lilith was not in the study when this took place. In justice to Teufelsbürst, it must be confessed that he employed all the skill he was master of, which for beneficent purposes was not very great, to restore the youth ; but without avail. At last, hearing the footsteps of Lilith, he desisted in some consternation ; and that she might escape being shocked by the sight of a dead body where she had been accustomed to see a living one, he removed the lay figure from the couch, and laid Karl in its place, covering him with the black velvet pall. He was just in time. She started at seeing no one in Karl's place, and said :

" Where is your pupil, father ? "

"Gone home," he answered, with a kind of convulsive grin.

She glanced round the room, caught sight of the lay figure where it had not been before, looked at the couch, and saw the pall yet heaved up from beneath, opened her eyes till the entire white sweep around the iris suggested a new expression of consternation to Teufelsbürst, though from a quarter whence he did not desire or !ook for it; and then, without a word, sat down to a drawing she had been busy upon the day before. But her father, glancing at her now, as Wolkenlicht had used to do, could not help seeing that she was frightfully pale. She showed no other sign of uneasiness. As soon as he released her, she withdrew, with one more glance, as she passed, at the couch and the figure blocked out in black upon it. She hastened to her chamber, shut and locked the door, sat down on the side of the couch, and fell, not a-weeping, but a-thinking. Was he dead? What did it matter? They would all be dead soon. Her mother was dead already. It was only that the earth could not bear more children, except she devoured those to whom she had already given birth. But what if they had to come back in another form, and live another sad, hopeless, loveless life over again?—And so she went on questioning, and receiving no replies; while through all her thoughts passed and re-passed the eyes of Wolkenlicht, which she had often felt to be upon her when she did not see them, wild with repressed longing, the light of their love shining through the veil of diffused tears, ever gathering and never overflowing. Then came the pale face, so worshipping, so distant in its self-withdrawn devotion, slowly dawning out of the vapours of her reverie. When it vanished, she tried to see it again. It would not come when she called it; but when her thoughts left knocking at the door of the lost and wandered away, out came the pale, troubled, silent face again, gathering itself up from some unknown nook in her world of phantasy, and once more, when she tried to steady it by the fixedness of her own regard, fading back into the mist. So the phantasm of the dead drew near and wooed, as the living had never dared.—What if there were any good in loving? What if men and women did not die all out, but some dim shade of each, like that pale, mind-ghost of Wolkenlicht, floated through the eternal vapours of chaos? And what if they might sometimes cross each other's path, meet, know that they met, love on? Would not that revive the withered memory, fix the fleeting ghost, give a new habitation, a body even, to the poor, unhoused wanderers, frozen by the eternal frosts, no longer thinking beings, but thoughts wandering through the brain of the "Melancholy Mass?" Back with the thought came the face of the dead Karl, and the maiden threw herself on her bed in a flood of bitter tears. She could have loved him if he had only lived : she did love him, for he was dead. But even in the midst of the remorse that followed,—for had she not killed him?—life seemed a less hard and hopeless thing than before. For it is love itself and not its responses or results that is the soul of life and its pleasures.

Two hours passed ere she could again show herself to her father, from whom she seemed in some new way divided by the new feeling in which he did not, and could not share. But at last, lest he should seek her, and finding her, should suspect her thoughts, she descended and sought him.—For there is a maidenliness in sorrow, that wraps her garments close around her.—But he was not to be seen; the door of the study was locked. A shudder passed through her as she thought of what her father, who lost no opportunity of furthering his all but perfect acquaintance with the human form and structure, might be about with the figure which she knew lay dead beneath that velvet pall, but which had arisen to haunt the hollow caves and cells of her living brain. She rushed away, and up once more to her silent room, through the darkness which had now settled down in the house; threw herself again on her bed, and lay almost paralysed with horror and distress.

But Teufelsbürst was not about anything so rightful as she supposed, though something frightful enough. I have already implied that Wolkenlicht was, in form, as fine an embodiment of youthful manhood as any old Greek republic could have provided one of its sculptors with as model for an Apollo. It is true, that to the eye of a Greek artist he would not have been more acceptable in consequence of the regimen he had been going through for the last few weeks; but the emaciation of Wolkenlicht's frame, and the consequent prominence of the muscles, indicating the pain he had gone through, were peculiarly attractive to Teufelsbürst.—He was busy preparing to take a cast of the body of his dead pupil, that it might aid to the perfection of his future labours.

He was deep in the artistic enjoyment of a form, at the same time so beautiful and strong, yet with the lines of suffering in every limb and feature, when his daughter's hand was laid on the latch. He started, flung the velvet drapery over the body, and went to the door.

But Lilith had vanished. He returned to his labours. The operation took a long time, for he performed it very carefully. Towards midnight, he had finished encasing the body in a close-clinging shell of plaster, which, when broken off, and fitted together, would be the matrix to the form of the dead Wolkenlicht. Before leaving it to harden till the morning, he was just proceeding to strengthen it with an additional layer all over, when a flash of lightning, reflected in all its dazzle from the snow without, almost blinded him. A peal of long-drawn thunder followed; the wind rose; and just such a storm came on as had risen some time before at the death of Kuntz, whose spectre was still torment-ing the city. The gnomes of terror, deep hidden in the caverns of Teufelsbürst's nature, broke out jubilant. With trembling hands he tried to cast the pall over the awful white chrysalis,—

failed, and fled to his chamber. And there lay the studio naked to the eyes of the lightning, with its tortured forms throbbing out of the dark, and quivering, as with life, in the almost continuous palpitations of the light; while on the couch lay the motionless mass of whiteness, gleaming blue in the lightning, almost more terrible in its crude indications of the human form, than that which it enclosed. It lay there as if dropped from some tree of chaos, haggard with the snows of eternity—a huge mis-shapen nut, with a corpse for its kernel.

But the lightning would soon have revealed a more terrible sight still, had there been any eyes to behold it. At midnight, while a peal of thunder was just dying away in the distance, the crust of death flew asunder, rending in all directions; and, pale as his investiture, staring with ghastly eyes, the form of Karl started up sitting on the couch. Had he not been far beyond ordinary men in strength, he could not thus have rent his sepulchre. Indeed, had Teufelsbürst been able to finish his task by the additional layer of gypsum which he contemplated, he must have died the moment life revived; although, so long as the trance lasted, neither the exclusion from the air, nor the practical solidification of the walls of his chest, could do him any injury. He had lain unconscious throughout the operations of Teufelsbürst, but now the catalepsy had passed away, possibly under the influence of the electric condition of the atmosphere. Very likely the strength he now put forth was intensified by a convulsive reaction of all the powers of life, as is not unfrequently the case in sudden awakenings from similar interruptions of vital activity. The coming to himself and the bursting of his case were simultaneous. He sat staring about him, with, of all his mental faculties, only his imagination awake, from which the thoughts that occupied it when he fell senseless had not yet faded. These thoughts had been compounded of feelings about Lilith, and speculations about the vampire that haunted the neighbourhood; and the fumes of the last drug of which he had partaken, still hovering in his brain, combined with these thoughts and fancies to generate the delusion that he had just broken from the embrace of his coffin, and risen, the last-born of the vampire-race. The sense of unavoidable obligation to fulfil his doom, was yet mingled with a faint flutter of joy, for he knew that he must go to Lilith. With a deep sigh, he rose, gathered up the pall of black velvet, flung it around him, stepped from the couch, and left the study to find her.

Meantime, Teufelsbürst had sufficiently recovered to remember that he had left the door of the studio unfastened, and that any one entering would discover in what he had been engaged which, in the case of his getting into any difficulty about the death of Karl, would tell powerfully against him. He was at the further end of a long passage, leading from the house to the studio, on his way to make all secure, when Karl appeared at the door, and advanced towards him. The painter, seized with invincible terror, turned and fled. He reached his room, and fell senseless on the floor. The phantom held on its way, heedless.

Lilith, on gaining her room the second time, had thrown herself on her bed as before, and had wept herself into a troubled slumber. She lay dreaming, and dreadful dreams. Suddenly she awoke in one of those peals of thunder which tormented the high regions of the air, as a storm billows the surface of the ocean. She lay awake and listened. As it died away, she thought she heard, mingling with its last muffled murmurs, the sound of moaning. She turned her face towards the room in keen terror. But she saw nothing. Another light, long-drawn sigh reached her ear, and at the same moment a flash of lightning illumined the room. In the corner farthest from her bed, she spied a white face, nothing more. She was dumb and motionless with fear. Utter darkness followed, a darkness that seemed to enter into her very brain. Yet she felt that the face was slowly crossing the black gulf of the room, and drawing near to where she lay. The next flash revealed, as it bended over her, the ghastly face of Karl, down which flowed fresh tears. The rest of his form was lost in blackness. Lilith did not faint, but it was the very force of her fear that seemed to keep her alive. It became for the moment the atmosphere of her life. She lay trembling and staring at the spot in the darkness where she supposed the face of Karl still to be. But the next flash showed her the face far off, looking at her through the panes of her lattice-window.

For Lottchen, as soon as he saw Lilith, seemed to himself to go through a second stage of awaking. Her face made him doubt whether he could be a vampire after all ; for instead of wanting to bite her arm and suck the blood, he all but fell down at her feet in a passion of speechless love. The next moment he became aware that his presence must be at least very undesirable to her ; and in an instant he had reached her window, which he knew looked upon a lower roof that extended between two different parts of the house, and before the next flash came, he had stepped through the lattice and closed it behind him.

Believing his own room to be attainable from this quarter, he proceeded along the roof in the direction he judged best. The cold winter air by degrees restored him entirely to his right mind, and he soon comprehended the whole of the circumstances in which he found himself. Peeping through a window he was passing, to see whether it belonged to his room, he spied Teufelsbürst, who, at the very moment, was lifting his head from the faint into which he had fallen at the first sight of Lottchen. The moon was shining clear, and in its light the painter saw, to his horror, the pale face staring in at his window. He thought it had been there ever since he had fainted, and dropped again in a deeper swoon than before. Karl saw him fall, and the truth flashed upon him that the wicked artist took him for what he had believed himself to be when first he recovered from his trance—namely, the vampire of the former Karl

Wolkenlicht. The moment he comprehended it, he resolved to keep up the delusion if possible. Meantime he was innocently preparing a new ingredient for the popular dish of horrors to be served at the ordinary of the city the next day. For the old servant's were not the only eyes that had seen him besides those of Teufelsbürst. What could be more like a vampire, dragging his pall after him, than this apparition of poor, half-frozen Lottchen, crawling across the roof? Karl remembered afterwards that he had heard the dogs howling awfully in every direction, as he crept along ; but this was hardly necessary to make those who saw him conclude that it was the same phantasm of John Kuntz, which had been infesting the whole city, and especially the house next door to the painter's, which had been the dwelling of the respectable alderman who had degenerated into this most disreputable of moneyless

vagabonds.   What added to the consternation of
all who heard of it, was the sickening conviction
that the extreme measures which they had re-
sorted to in order to free the city from the ghoul,
beyond which nothing could be done, had been
utterly unavailing, successful as they had proved
in every other known case of the kind.   For,
urged as well by various horrid signs about his
grave, which not even its close proximity to the
altar could render a place of repose, they had
opened it, had found in the body every peculiarity
belonging to a vampire, had pulled it out with the
greatest difficulty on account of a quite super-
natural ponderosity; which rendered the horse
which had killed him—a strong animal—all but
unable to drag it along, and had at last, after
cutting it in pieces, and expending on the fire two
hundred and sixteen great billets, succeeded in
conquering its incombustibleness, and reducing it

to ashes. Such, at least, was the story which had reached the painter's household, and was believed by many; and if all this did not compel the per-turbed corpse to rest, what more could be done?

When Karl had reached his room, and was dressing himself, the thought struck him that something might be made of the report of the extreme weight of the body of old Kuntz, to favour the continuance of the delusion of Teufelsbürst, although he hardly knew yet to what use he could turn this delusion. He was convinced that he would have made no progress however long he might have remained in his house; and that he would have more chance of favour with Lilith if he were to meet her in any other circumstances whatever, than those in which he invariably saw her—namely, surrounded by her father's influences, and watched by her father's cold blue eyes.

As soon as he was dressed, he crept down to

the studio, which was now quiet enough, the storm being over, and the moon filling it with her steady shine. In the corner lay in all directions the fragments of the mould which his own body had formed and filled. The bag of plaster and the bucket of water which the painter had been using stood beside. Lottchen gathered all the pieces together, and then making his way to an out-house where he had seen various odds and ends of rubbish lying, chose from the heap as many pieces of old iron and other metal as he could find. To these he added a few large stones from the garden. When he had got all into the studio, he locked the door, and proceeded to fit together the parts of the mould, filling up the hollow as he went on with the heaviest things he could get into it, and solidifying the whole by pouring in plaster; till, having at length completed it, and obliterated, as much as possible, the marks of joining, he left it to harden, with the conviction that now it would make a considerable impression on Teufelsbürst's imagination, as well as on his muscular sense. He then left everything else as nearly undisturbed as he could; and, knowing all the ways of the house, was soon in the street, without leaving any signs of his exit.

Karl soon found himself before the house in which his friend Höllenrachen resided. Knowing his studious habits, he had hoped to see his light still burning, nor was he disappointed. He contrived to bring him to his window, and a moment after, the door was cautiously opened.

" Why, Lottchen, where do you come from ? "

" From the grave, Heinrich, or next door to it."

" Come in, and tell me all about it. We thought the old painter had made a model of you, and tortured you to death."

" Perhaps you were not far wrong. But get me

a horn of ale, for even a vampire is thirsty, you know."

" A vampire ! " exclaimed Heinrich, retreating a pace, and involuntarily putting himself upon his guard.

Karl laughed.

" My hand was warm, was it not, old fellow ? " he said.   " Vampires are cold, all but the blood."

" What a fool I am ! " rejoined Heinrich. " But you know we have been hearing such horrors lately that a fellow may be excused for shuddering a little when a pale-faced apparition tells him at two o'clock in the morning that he is a vampire, and thirsty, too."

Karl told him the whole story ; and the mental process of regarding it for the sake of telling it, revealed to him pretty clearly some of the treat-ment of which he had been unconscious at the time.   Heinrich was quite sure that his suspicions were correct. And now the question was, what was to be done next.

" At all events," said Heinrich, "we must keep you out of the way for some time. I will represent to my landlady that you are in hiding from enemies, and her heart will rule her tongue. She can let you have a garret-room, I know; and I will do as well as I can to bear you company. We shall have time then to invent some plan of operation."

To this proposal Karl agreed with hearty thanks, and soon all was arranged. The only conclusion they could yet arrive at was, that somehow or other the old demon-painter must be tamed.

Meantime, how fared it with Lilith? She too had no doubt that she had seen the body-ghost of poor Karl, and that the vampire had, according to rule, paid her the first visit because he loved her best. This was horrible enough if the vampire were not really the person he represented ; but if in any sense it were Karl himself, at least it gave some expectation of a more prolonged existence than her father had taught her to look for ; and if love anything like her mother's still lasted, even along with the habits of a vampire, there was something to hope for in the future. And then, though he had visited her, he had not, as far as she was aware, deprived her of a drop of blood. She could not be certain that he had not bitten her, for she had been in such a strange condition of mind that she might not have felt it, but she believed that he had restrained the impulses of his vampire nature, and had left her, lest he should yet yield to them. She fell fast asleep ; and, when morning came, there was not, as far as she could judge, one of those triangular leech-like perforations to be found upon her whole body.

Will it be believed that the moment she was satisfied of this, she was seized by a terrible jealousy, lest Karl should have gone and bitten some one else? Most people will wonder that she should not have gone out of her senses at once; but there was all the difference between a visit from a real vampire and a visit from a man she had begun to love, even although she took him for a vampire. All the difference does *not* lie in a name. They were very different causes, and the effects must be very different.

When Teufelsbürst came down in the morning, he crept into the studio like a murderer. There lay the awful white block, seeming to his eyes just the same as he had left it. What was to be done with it? He dared not open it. Mould and model must go together. But whither? If inquiry should be made after Wolkenlicht, and this were discovered anywhere on his premises, would it not be enough to bring him at once to the gallows? Therefore it would be dangerous to bury it in the garden; or in the cellar.

"Besides," thought he, with a shudder, "that would be to fix the vampire as a guest for ever." —And the horrors of the past night rushed back upon his imagination with renewed intensity. What would it be to have the dead Karl crawling about his house for ever, now inside, now out, now sitting on the stairs, now staring in at the windows?

He would have dragged it to the bottom of his garden, past which the Moldau flowed, and plunged it into the stream; but then, should the spectre continue to prove troublesome, it would be almost impossible to reach the body so as to destroy it by fire; besides which, he could not do it without assistance, and the probability of discovery. If, however, the apparition should turn out to be no vampire, but only a respectable ghost, they might manage to endure its presence, till it should be weary of haunting them.

He resolved at last to convey the body for the meantime into a concealed cellar in the house, seeing something must be done before his daughter came down. Proceeding to remove it, his consternation was greatly increased when he discovered how the body had grown in weight since he had thus disposed of it, leaving on his mind scarcely a hope that it could turn out not to be a vampire after all. He could scarcely stir it, and there was but one whom he could call to his assistance—the old woman who acted as his housekeeper and servant.

He went to her room, roused her, and told her the whole story. Devoted to her master for many years, and not quite so sensitive to fearful influences as when less experienced in horrors, she showed immediate readiness to render him assistance. Utterly unable, however, to lift the mass between them, they could only drag and push it along; and such a slow toil was it that there was no time to remove the traces of its track, before Lilith came down and saw a broad white line leading from the door of the studio down the cellar-stairs. She knew in a moment what it meant; but not a word was uttered about the matter, and the name of Karl Wolkenlicht seemed to be entirely forgotten.

But how could the affairs of a house go on all the same when every one of the household knew that a dead body lay in the cellar?—nay more, that, although it lay still and dead enough all day, it would come half alive at nightfall, and, turning the whole house into a sepulchre by its presence, go creeping about like a cat all over it in the dark—perhaps with phosphorescent eyes? So it was not surprising that the painter abandoned his studio early, and that the three found themselves together in the gorgeous room formerly described, as soon as twilight began to fall.

Already Teufelsbürst had begun to experience a kind of shrinking from the horrid faces in his own pictures, and to feel disgusted at the abortions of his own mind. But all that he and the old woman now felt was an increasing fear as the night drew on, a kind of sickening and paralysing terror. The thing down there would not lie quiet—at least its phantom in the cellars of their imagination would not. As much as possible, however, they avoided alarming Lilith, who, knowing all they knew, was as silent as they. But her mind was in a strange state of excitement, partly from the presence of a new sense of love, the pleasure of which all the atmosphere of grief into which it grew could not totally quench. It comforted her somehow, as a child may comfort when his father is away.

Bedtime came and no one made a move to go. Without a word spoken on the subject, the three remained together all night ; the elders nodding and slumbering occasionally, and Lilith getting some share of repose on a couch. All night the shape of death might be somewhere about the house ; but it did not disturb them. They heard no sound, saw no sight ; and when the morning dawned, they separated, chilled and stupid, and for the time beyond fear, to seek repose in their private chambers. There they remained equally undisturbed.

But when the painter approached his easel a few hours after, looking more pale and haggard still than he was wont, from the fears of the night, a new bewilderment took possession of him. He had been busy with a fresh embodiment of his

favourite subject, into which he had sketched the
form of the student as the sufferer. He had
represented poor Wolkenlicht as just beginning
to recover from a trance, while a group of
surgeons, unaware of the signs of returning life,
were absorbed in a minute dissection of one of the
limbs. At an open door he had painted Lilith
passing, with her face buried in a bunch of sweet-
peas. But when he came to the picture, he found
to his astonishment and terror, that the face of
one of the group was now turned towards that of
the victim, regarding his revival with demoniac
satisfaction, and taking pains to prevent the others
from discovering it. The face of this prince of
torturers was that of Teufelsbürst himself. Lilith
had altogether vanished, and in her place stood
the dim vampire reiteration of the body that lay
extended on the table, staring greedily at the
assembled company. With trembling hands the

painter removed the picture from the easel, and turned its face to the wall.

Of course this was the work of Lottchen. When he left the house, he took with him the key of a small private door, which was so seldom used that, while it remained closed, the key would not be missed, perhaps for many months. Watching the windows, he had chosen a safe time to enter, and had been hard at work all night on these alterations. Teufelsbürst attributed them to the vampire, and left the picture as he found it, not daring to put brush to it again.

The next night was passed much after the same fashion. But the fear had begun to die away a little in the hearts of the women, who did not know what had taken place in the study on the previous night. It burrowed, however, with gathered force in the vitals of Teufelsbürst. But this night likewise passed in peace ; and before it was over, the old woman had taken to speculating in her own mind as to the best way of disposing of the body, seeing it was not at all likely to be troublesome. But when the painter entered his study in trepidation the next morning, he found that the form of the lovely Lilith was painted out of every picture in the room. This could not be concealed; and Lilith and the servant became aware that the studio was the portion of the house in haunting which the vampire left the rest in peace.

Karl recounted all the tricks he had played to ais friend Heinrich, who begged to be allowed to bear him company the following night. To this Karl consented, thinking it would be considerably more agreeable to have a companion. So they took a couple of bottles of wine and some provisions with them, and before midnight found themselves snug in the study. They sat very quiet for some time, for they knew that if they were seen, two vampires would not be so terrible as one, and might occasion discovery. But at length Heinrich could bear it no longer.

"I say, Lottchen, let's go and look for your dead body. What has the old beggar done with it?"

"I think I know. Stop; let me peep out. All right! Come along."

With a lamp in his hand, he led the way to the cellars, and after searching about a little, they discovered it.

"It looks horrid enough," said Heinrich, "but I think a drop or two of wine would brighten it up a little."

So he took a bottle from his pocket, and after they had had a glass apiece, he dropped a third in blots all over the plaster. Being red wine, it had the effect Höllenrachen desired.

" When they visit it next, they will know that the vampire can find the food he prefers," said he.

In a corner close by the plaster, they found the clothes Karl had worn.

" Hillo !" said Heinrich, "we'll make something of this find."

So he carried them with him to the study. There he got hold of the lay-figure.

" What are you about, Heinrich? "

" Going to make a scarecrow to keep the ravens off old Teufel's pictures," answered Heinrich, as he went on dressing the lay-figure in Karl's clothes. He next seated the creature at an easel with its back to the door, so that it should be the first thing the painter should see when he entered. Karl meant to remove this before he went, for it was too comical to fall in with the rest of his proceedings. But the two sat down to their supper, and by the time they had finished the wine, they thought they should like to go to bed. So they got up and went home, and Karl forgot the lay-figure, leaving it in busy motionlessness all night before the easel.

When Teufelsbürst saw it, he turned and fled with a cry that brought his daughter to his help. He rushed past her, able only to articulate:

"The vampire! The vampire! Painting!"

Far more courageous than he, because her conscience was more peaceful, Lilith passed on to the study. She too recoiled a step or two when she saw the figure; but with the sight of the back of Karl, as she supposed it to be, came the longing to see the face that was on the other side. So she crept round and round by the wall, as far off as she could. The figure remained motionless. It was a strange kind of shock that she experienced when she saw the face, disgusting from its inanity. The absurdity next struck her; and with the absurdity flashed into her mind the conviction that this was not the doing of a vampire; for of all creatures under the moon, he could not be expected to be a humourist. A wild hope sprang up in her mind that Karl was not dead. Of this she soon resolved to make herself sure.

She closed the door of the study; in the strength of her new hope, undressed the figure, put it in its place, concealed the garments—all the work of a few minutes; and then, finding her father just recovering from the worst of his fear, told him there was nothing in the study but what ought to be there, and persuaded him to go and see. He not only saw no one, but found that no further liberties had been taken with his pictures. Re-assured, he soon persuaded himself that the spectre in this case had been the offspring of his own terror-haunted brain. But he had no spirit for painting now. He wandered about the house, himself haunting it like a restless ghost.

When night came, Lilith retired to her own room. The waters of fear had begun to subside in the house; but the painter and his old attendant did not yet follow her example.

As soon, however, as the house was quite still, Lilith glided noiselessly down the stairs, went into the study, where as yet there assuredly was no vampire, and concealed herself in a corner.

As it would not do for an earnest student like Heinrich to be away from his work very often, he had not asked to accompany Lottchen this time. And indeed Karl himself, a little anxious about the result of the scarecrow, greatly preferred going alone.

While she was waiting for what might happen, the conviction grew upon Lilith, as she reviewed all the past of the story, that these phenomena were the work of the real Karl, and of no vampire. In a few moments she was still more sure of this. Behind the screen where she had taken refuge, hung one of the pictures out of which her portrait had been painted the night before last. She had taken a lamp with her into the study, with the intention of extinguishing it the moment she heard any sign of approach; but as the vampire lingered, she began to occupy herself with examining the picture beside her. She had not looked at it long, before she wetted the tip of her forefinger, and began to rub away at the obliteration. Her suspicions were instantly confirmed: the substance employed was only a gummy wash over the paint. The delight she experienced at the discovery threw her into a mischievous humour.

"I will see," she said to herself, "whether I cannot match Karl Wolkenlicht at this game."

In a closet in the room hung a number of

costumes, which Lilith had at different times worn
for her father.   Among them was a large white
drapery, which she easily disposed as a shroud.
With the help of some chalk, she soon made
herself ghastly enough, and then placing her lamp
on the floor behind the screen, and setting a chair
over it, so that it should throw no light in any
direction, she waited once more for the vampire.
Nor had she much longer to wait. She soon heard
a door move, the sound of which she hardly knew,
and then the study door opened.   Her heart beat
dreadfully, not with fear lest it should be a vampire
after all, but with hope that it was Karl.   To see
him once more was too great joy.   Would she not
make up to him for all her coldness!   But would
he care for her now?   Perhaps he had been quite
cured of his longing for a hard heart like hers.
She peeped.   It was he sure enough, looking as
handsome as ever.   He was holding his light to

look at her last work, and the expression of his face, even in regarding her handiwork, was enough to let her know that he loved her still. If she had not seen this, she dared not have shown herself from her hiding-place. Taking the lamp in her hand, she got upon the chair, and looked over the screen, letting the light shine from below upon her face. She then made a slight noise to attract Karl's attention. He looked up, evidently rather startled, and saw the face of Lilith in the air. He gave a stifled cry, threw himself on his knees, with his arms stretched towards her, and moaned :

" I have killed her ! I have killed her ! "

Lilith descended, and approached him noise-lessly. He did not move. She came close to him and said :

" Are you Karl Wolkenlicht ? "

His lips moved, but no sound came.

" If you are a vampire, and I am a ghost," she

said—but a low happy laugh alone concluded the sentence.

Karl sprang to his feet. Lilith's laugh changed into a burst of sobbing and weeping, and in another moment the ghost was in the arms of the vampire.

Lilith had no idea how far her father had wronged Karl, and though, from thinking over the past, he had no doubt that the painter had drugged him, he did not wish to pain her by imparting this conviction. But Lilith was afraid of a reaction of rage and hatred in her father after the terror was removed; and Karl saw that he might thus be deprived of all further intercourse with Lilith, and all chance of softening the old man's heart towards him; while Lilith would not hear of forsaking him who had banished all the human race but herself. They managed at length to agree upon a plan of operation.

The first thing they did was to go to the cellar where the plaster mass lay, Karl carrying with him a great axe used for cleaving wood. Lilith shuddered when she saw it, stained as it was with the wine Heinrich had spilt over it, and almost believed herself the midnight companion of a vampire after all, visiting with him the terrible corpse in which he lived all day. But Karl soon reassured her; and a few good blows of the axe revealed a very different core to that which Teufels-bürst supposed to be in it. Karl broke it into pieces, and with Lilith's help, who insisted on carrying her share, the whole was soon at the bottom of the Moldau, and every trace of its ever having existed removed. Before morning, too, the form of Lilith had dawned anew in every picture. There was no time to restore to its former condi-tion the one Karl had first altered; for in it the changes were all that they seemed; nor indeed

was he capable of restoring it in the master's style;
but they put it quite out of the way, and hoped
that sufficient time might elapse before the painter
thought of it again.

When they had done, and Lilith, for all his
entreaties, would remain with him no longer, Karl
took his former clothes with him, and having
spent the rest of the night in his old room, dressed
in them in the morning.   When Teufelsbürst
entered his study next day, there sat Karl, as if
nothing had happened, finishing the drawing on
which he had been at work when the fit of insensibility came upon him.   The painter started, stared,
rubbed his eyes, thought it was another spectral
illusion, but was on the point of yielding to his
terror, when Karl rose, and approached him with
a smile.   The healthy, sunshiny countenance of
Karl, let him be ghost or goblin, could not fail to
produce somewhat of a tranquillizing effect on

Teufelsbürst.   He took his offered hand mechanically, his countenance utterly vacant with
idiotic bewilderment.   Karl said:

" I was not well, and thought it better to pay a
visit to a friend for a few days; but I shall soon
make up for lost time, for I am all right now."

He sat down at once, taking no notice of his
master's behaviour, and went on with his drawing.
Teufelsbürst stood staring at him for some minutes
without moving, then suddenly turned and left the
room.   Karl heard him hurrying down the cellar
stairs.   In a few moments he came up again.
Karl stole a glance at him.   There he stood in
the same spot, no doubt more full of bewilderment
than ever; but it was not possible that his face
should express more.   At last he went to his
easel, and sat down with a long-drawn sigh as if of
relief.   But though he sat at his easel, he painted
none that day; and as often as Karl ventured a

glance, he saw him still staring at him. The discovery that his pictures were restored to their former condition aided, no doubt, in leading him to the same conclusion as the other facts, whatever that conclusion might be—probably that he had been the sport of some evil power, and had been for the greater part of a week utterly bewitched. Lilith had taken care to instruct the old woman, with whom she was all-powerful; and as neither of them showed the smallest traces of the astonishment which seemed to be slowly vitrifying his own brain, he was at last perfectly satisfied that things had been going on all right everywhere but in his inner man; and in this conclusion he certainly was not far wrong in more senses than one. But when all was restored again to the old routine, it became evident that the peculiar direction of his art in which he had hitherto indulged had ceased to interest him. The shock had acted chiefly upon that part of his mental being which had been so absorbed. He would sit for hours without doing anything, apparently plunged in meditation.— Several weeks elapsed without any change, and both Lilith and Karl were getting dreadfully anxious about him. Karl paid him every attention; and the old man, for he now looked much older than before, submitted to receive his services as well as those of Lilith. At length, one morning, he said in a slow thoughtful tone:

"Karl Wolkenlicht, I should like to paint you."

"Certainly, sir," answered Karl, jumping up, "where would you like me to sit?"

So the ice of silence and inactivity was broken, and the painter drew and painted; and the spring of his art flowed once more; and he made a beautiful portrait of Karl; a portrait without evil or suffering. And as soon as he had finished Karl, he began once more to paint Lilith; and when he had painted her, he composed a picture for the very purpose of introducing them together; and in this picture there was neither ugliness nor torture, but human feeling and human hope instead. Then Karl knew that he might speak to him of Lilith; and he spoke, and was heard with a smile. But he did not dare to tell him the truth of the vampire story till one day that Teufelsbürst was lying on the floor of a room in Karl's ancestral castle, half smothered in grand-children; when the only answer it drew from the old man was a kind of shuddering laugh, and the words—" Don't speak of it, Karl, my boy!"

THE CASTLE:

A PARABLE.

THE CASTLE.

ON the top of a high cliff, forming part of the base of a great mountain, stood a lofty castle. When or how it was built, no man knew; nor could any one pretend to understand its architecture. Every one who looked upon it felt that it was lordly and noble; and where one part seemed not to agree with another, the wise and modest dared not to call them incongruous, but presumed that the whole might be constructed on some higher principle of architecture than they yet understood. What helped them to this conclusion was, that no one had ever seen the whole of the edifice; that, even of the portion best known, some part or other was always wrapt in thick folds of mist from the mountain; and that, when the sun shone upon this mist, the parts of the building that appeared through the vaporous veil, were strangely glorified in their indistinctness, so that they seemed to belong to some aerial abode in the land of the sunset; and the beholders could hardly tell whether they had ever seen them before, or whether they were now for the first time partially revealed.

Nor, although it was inhabited, could certain information be procured as to its internal construction. Those who dwelt in it often discovered rooms they had never entered before; yea, once or twice, whole suites of apartments, of which only dim legends had been handed down from former times. Some of them expected to find, one day, secret places, filled with treasures of wondrous jewels; amongst which they hoped to light upon Solomon's ring, which had for ages disappeared from the earth, but which had controlled the spirits, and the possession of which made a man simply what a man should be, the king of the world. Now and then, a narrow, winding stair, hitherto untrodden, would bring them forth on a new turret, whence new prospects of the circumjacent country were spread out before them. How many more of these there might be, or how much loftier, no one could tell. Nor could the foundations of the castle in the rock on which it was built be determined with the smallest approach to precision. Those of the family who had given themselves to exploring in that direction, found such a labyrinth of vaults and passages, and endless successions of down-going stairs, out of one underground space into a yet lower, that they came to the conclusion that at least the whole mountain was perforated and honeycombed in this fashion. They had a dim consciousness, too, of the presence, in those awful regions, of beings whom they could not comprehend. Once, they came upon the brink of a great black gulf, in which the eye could see nothing but darkness: they recoiled with horror; for the conviction flashed upon them that that gulf went down into the very central spaces of the earth, of which they had hitherto been wandering only in the upper crust; nay, that the seething blackness before them had relations mysterious, and beyond human comprehension, with the far-off voids of space, into which the stars dare not enter.

At the foot of the cliff whereon the castle stood, lay a deep lake, inaccessible save by a few avenues, being surrounded on all sides with precipices, which made the water look very black, although it was pure as the night-sky. From a door in the castle, which was not to be otherwise entered, a broad flight of steps, cut in the rock, went down to the lake, and disappeared below its surface. Some thought the steps went to the very bottom of the water.

Now in this castle there dwelt a large family of brothers and sisters. They had never seen their father or mother. The younger had been educated by the elder, and these by an unseen care and ministration, about the sources of which they had, somehow or other, troubled themselves very little, for what people are accustomed to, they regard as coming from nobody; as if help and progress and joy and love were the natural crops of Chaos or old Night. But Tradition said that one day—it was utterly uncertain *when*—their father would come, and leave them no more; for he was still alive, though where he lived nobody knew. In the meantime all the rest had to obey their eldest brother, and listen to his counsels.

But almost all the family was very fond of liberty, as they called it; and liked to run up and down, hither and thither, roving about, with neither law nor order, just as they pleased. So they could not endure their brother's tyranny, as they called it. At one time they said that he was only one of themselves, and therefore they would not obey him; at another, that he was not like them, and could not understand them, and *therefore* they would not obey him. Yet, sometimes, when he came and looked them full in the face, they were terrified, and dared not disobey, for he was stately, and stern and strong. Not one of them loved him heartily, except the eldest sister, who was very beautiful and silent, and whose eyes shone as if light lay somewhere deep behind them. Even she, although she loved him, thought him very hard sometimes; for when he had once said a thing plainly, he could not be persuaded to think it over again. So even she forgot him sometimes, and went her own ways, and enjoyed herself without him. Most of them regarded him as a sort of watchman, whose business it was to keep them in order; and so they were indignant and disliked him. Yet they all had a secret feeling that they ought to be subject to him; and after any particular act of disregard, none of them could think, with any peace, of the old story about the return of their father to his house. But indeed they never thought much about it, or about their father at all; for how could those who cared so little for their brother, whom they saw every day, care for their father whom they had never seen?—One chief cause of complaint against him was, that he interfered with their favourite studies and pursuits; whereas he only sought to make them give up trifling with earnest things, and seek for truth, and not for amusement, from the many wonders around them. He did not want them to turn to other studies, or to eschew pleasures; but, in those studies, to seek the highest things most, and other things in proportion to their true worth and nobleness. This could not fail to be distasteful to those who did not care for what was higher than they. And so matters went on for a time. They thought they could do better without their brother; and their brother knew they could not do at all without him, and tried to fulfil the charge committed into his hands.

At length, one day, for the thought seemed to strike them simultaneously, they conferred together about giving a great entertainment in their grandest rooms to any of their neighbours who chose to come, or indeed to any inhabitants of the earth or air who would visit them. They were too proud to reflect that some company might defile even the dwellers in what was undoubtedly the finest palace on the face of the earth. But what made the thing worse, was, that the old tradition said that these rooms were to be kept entirely for the use of the owner of the castle. And, indeed, whenever they entered them, such was the effect of their loftiness and grandeur upon their minds, that they always thought of the old story, and could not help believing it. Nor would the brother permit them to forget it now; but, appearing suddenly amongst them, when they had no expectation of being interrupted by him, he rebuked them, both for the indiscriminate nature of their invitation, and for the intention of intro- ducing any one, not to speak of some who would doubtless make their appearance on the evening in question, into the rooms kept sacred for the use of the unknown father. But by this time their talk with each other had so excited their expectations of enjoyment, which had previously been strong enough, that anger sprung up within them at the thought of being deprived of their hopes, and they looked each other in the eyes ; and the look said: " We are many, and he is one—let us get rid of him, for he is always finding fault, and thwarting us in the most innocent pleasures ;—as if we would wish to do anything wrong!" So without a word spoken, they rushed upon him ; and although he was stronger than any of them, and struggled hard at first, yet they overcame him at last.   Indeed some of them thought he yielded to their violence long before they had the mastery of him ; and this very submission terrified the more tender-hearted among them.   However, they bound him ; carried him down many stairs, and, having remembered an iron staple in the wall of a certain vault, with a thick rusty chain attached to it, they bore him thither, and made the chain fast around him. There they left him. shutting the great gnarring brazen door of the vault, as they departed for the upper regions of the castle.

Now all was in a tumult of preparation. Every one was talking of the coming festivity; but no one spoke of the deed they had done. A sudden paleness overspread the face, now of one, and now of another; but it passed away, and no one took any notice of it; they only plied the task of the moment the more energetically. Messengers were sent far and near, not to individuals or families, but publishing in all places of concourse a general invitation to any who chose to come on a certain day, and partake for certain succeeding days, of the hospitality of the dwellers in the castle. Many were the preparations immediately begun for complying with the invitation. But the noblest of their neighbours refused to appear; not from pride, but because of the unsuitableness and carelessness of such a mode.   With some of them it was an old condition in the tenure of their estates, that they should go to no one's dwelling except visited in person, and expressly solicited. Others, knowing what sort of persons would be there, and that, from a certain physical antipathy, they could scarcely breathe in their company, made up their minds at once not to go.   Yet multitudes, many of them beautiful and innocent as well as gay, resolved to appear.

Meanwhile the great rooms of the castle were got in readiness — that is, they proceeded to deface them with decorations; for there was a solemnity and stateliness about them in their ordinary condition, which was at once felt to be unsuitable for the light-hearted company so soon to move about in them with the self-same care- lessness with which men walk abroad within the great heavens and hills and clouds. One day, while the workmen were busy, the eldest sister, of whom I have already spoken, happened to enter, she knew not why. Suddenly the great idea of the mighty halls dawned upon her, and filled her soul. The so-called decorations vanished from her view, and she felt as if she stood in her father's presence. She was at once elevated and humbled. As suddenly the idea faded and fled, and she beheld but the gaudy festoons and draperies and paintings which disfigured the grandeur. She wept and sped away. Now it was too late to interfere, and things must take their course. She would have been but a Cassandra-prophetess to those who saw but the pleasure before them. She had not been present when her brother was imprisoned; and indeed for some days had been so wrapt in her own business, that she had taken but little heed of anything that was going on. But they all expected her to show herself when the company was gathered; and they had applied to her for advice at various times during their operations.

At length the expected hour arrived, and the company began to assemble. It was a warm summer evening. The dark lake reflected the rose-coloured clouds in the west, and through the flush rowed many gaily-painted boats, with various coloured flags, towards the massy rock on which the castle stood. The trees and flowers seemed already asleep, and breathing forth their sweet dream-breath. Laughter and low voices rose from the breast of the lake to the ears of the youths and maidens looking forth expectant from the lofty windows. They went down to the broad platform at the top of the stairs in front of the door to receive their visitors. By degrees the festivities of the evening commenced. The same smiles flew forth both at eyes and lips, darting like beams through the gathering crowd. Music, from unseen sources, now rolled in billows, now crept in ripples through the sea of air that filled the lofty rooms. And in the dancing halls, when hand took hand, and form and motion were moulded and swayed by the indwelling music, it governed not these alone, but, as the ruling spirit of the place, every new burst of music for a new dance swept before it a new and accordant odour, and dyed the flames that glowed in the lofty lamps with a new and accordant stain. The floors bent beneath the feet of the time-keeping dancers. But twice in the evening some of the inmates started, and the pallor occasionally common to the household overspread their faces, for they felt underneath them a counter-motion to the dance, as if the floor rose slightly to answer their feet. And all the time their brother lay below in the dungeon, like John the Baptist in the castle of Herod, when the lords and captains sat around, and the daughter of Herodias danced before them. Outside, all around the castle, brooded the dark night unheeded; for the clouds had come up from all sides, and were crowding together overhead. In the unfrequent pauses of the music, they might have heard, now and then, the gusty rush of a lonely wind, coming and going no one could know whence or whither, born and dying unexpected and unregarded.

But when the festivities were at their height, when the external and passing confidence which is produced between superficial natures by a common pleasure, was at the full, a sudden crash of thunder quelled the music, as the thunder quells the noise of the uplifted sea. The windows were driven in, and torrents of rain, carried in the folds of a rushing wind, poured into the halls.

The lights were swept away; and the great rooms, now dark within, were darkened yet more by the dazzling shoots of flame from the vault of blackness overhead. Those that ventured to look out of the windows saw, in the blue brilliancy of the quick-following jets of lightning, the lake at the foot of the rock, ordinarily so still and so dark, lighted up, not on the surface only, but down to half its depth; so that, as it tossed in the wind like a tortured sea of writhing flames, or incandescent half-molten serpents of brass, they could not tell whether a strong phosphorescence did not issue from the transparent body of the waters, as if earth and sky lightened together, one consenting source of flaming utterance.

Sad was the condition of the late plastic mass of living form that had flowed into shape at the will and law of the music. Broken into individuals, the common transfusing spirit withdrawn, they stood drenched, cold, and benumbed, with clinging garments; light, order, harmony, purpose departed, and chaos restored; the issuings of life turned back on their sources, chilly and dead. And in every heart reigned that falsest of despairing convictions, that this was the only reality, and that was but a dream. The eldest sister stood with clasped hands and down-bent head, shivering and speechless, as if waiting for something to follow. Nor did she wait long. A terrible flash and thunder-peal made the castle rock; and in the pausing silence that followed, her quick sense heard the rattling of a chain far off, deep down; and soon the sound of heavy footsteps, accompanied with the clanking of iron reached her ear. She felt that her brother was at hand. Even in the darkness, and amidst the bellowing of another deep-bosomed cloud-monster, she knew that he had entered the room. A moment after, a continuous pulsation of angry blue light began, which, lasting for some moments, revealed him standing amidst them, gaunt, haggard, and motionless; his hair and beard untrimmed, his face ghastly, his eyes large and hollow. The light seemed to gather around him as a centre. Indeed some believed that it throbbed and radiated from his person, and not from the stormy heavens above them. The lightning had rent the wall of his prison, and released the iron staple of his chain, which he had wound about him like a girdle. In his hand he carried an iron fetter-bar, which he had found on the floor of the vault. More terrified at his aspect than at all the violence of the storm, the visitors, with many a shriek and cry, rushed out into the tempestuous night. By degrees, the storm died away. Its last flash revealed the forms of the brothers and sisters lying prostrate, with their faces on the floor, and that fearful shape standing motionless amidst them still.

Morning dawned, and there they lay, and there he stood. But at a word from him, they arose and went about their various duties, though listlessly enough. The eldest sister was the last to rise; and when she did, it was only by a terrible effort that she was able to reach her room, where she fell again on the floor. There she remained lying for days. The brother caused the doors of the great suite of rooms to be closed, leaving them just as they were, with all the childish adornment scattered about, and the rain still falling in through the shattered windows. "Thus let them lie," said he, "till the rain and frost have cleansed them of paint and drapery: no storm can hurt the pillars and arches of these halls."

The hours of this day went heavily. The storm was gone, but the rain was left; the passion had departed, but the tears remained behind. Dull and dark the low misty clouds brooded over the castle and the lake, and shut out all the neighbourhood. Even if they had climbed to the loftiest known turret, they would have found it swathed in a garment of clinging vapour, affording no refreshment to the eye, and no hope to the heart. There was one lofty tower that rose sheer a hundred feet above the rest, and from which the fog could have been seen lying in a grey mass beneath; but that tower they had not yet discovered, nor another close beside it, the top of which was never seen, nor could be, for the highest clouds of heaven clustered continually around it. The rain fell continuously, though not heavily, without; and within, too, there were clouds from which dropped the tears which are the rain of the spirit. All the good of life seemed for the time departed, and their souls lived but as leafless trees that had forgotten the joy of the summer, and whom no wind prophetic of spring had yet visited. They moved about mechanically, and had not strength enough left to wish to die.

The next day the clouds were higher, and a little wind blew through such loopholes in the turrets as the false improvements of the inmates had not yet filled with glass, shutting out, as the storm, so the serene visitings of the heavens. Throughout the day, the brother took various opportunities of addressing a gentle command, now to one and now to another of his family. It was obeyed in silence. The wind blew fresher through the loopholes and the shattered windows of the great rooms, and found its way, by un-known passages, to faces and eyes hot with weeping. It cooled and blessed them.—When he sun arose the next day, it was in a clear sky.

By degrees, everything fell into the regularity of subordination. With the subordination came increase of freedom. The steps of the more youthful of the family were heard on the stairs and in the corridors more light and quick than ever before. Their brother had lost the terrors of aspect produced by his confinement, and his commands were issued more gently, and oftener with a smile, than in all their previous history. By degrees his presence was universally felt through the house. It was no surprise to any one at his studies, to see him by his side when he lifted up his eyes, though he had not before known that he was in the room. And although some dread still remained, it was rapidly vanishing before the advances of a firm friendship. Without immediately ordering their labours, he always influenced them, and often altered their direction and objects. The change soon evident in the household was remarkable. A simpler, nobler expression was visible on all the countenances. The voices of the men were deeper, and yet seemed by their very depth more feminine than before; while the voices of the women were softer and sweeter, and at the same time more full and decided. Now the eyes had often an expression as if their sight was absorbed in the gaze of the inward eyes; and when the eyes of two met, there passed between those eyes the utterance of a conviction that both meant the same thing. But the change was, of course, to be seen more clearly, though not more evidently, in individuals.

One of the brothers, for instance, was very fond of astronomy. He had his observatory on a lofty tower, which stood pretty clear of the others, towards the north and east. But hitherto, his astronomy, as he had called it, had been more of the character of astrology. Often, too, he might

have been seen directing a heaven - searching
telescope to catch the rapid transit of a fiery
shooting-star, belonging altogether to the earthly
atmosphere, and not to the serene heavens. He
had to learn that the signs of the air are not the
signs of the skies. Nay, once, his brother sur-
prised him in the act of examining through ·his
longest tube a patch of burning heath upon a
distant hill. But now he was diligent from
morning till night in the study of the laws of
the truth that has to do with stars ; and when the
curtain of the sun-light was about to rise from
before the heavenly worlds which it had hidden
all day long, he might be seen preparing his
instruments with that solemn countenance with
which it becometh one to look into the mysterious
harmonies of Nature. Now he learned what law
and order and truth are, what consent and
harmony mean ; how the individual may find his

own end in a higher end, where law and freedom mean the same thing, and the purest certainty exists without the slightest constraint. Thus he stood on the earth, and looked to the heavens.

Another, who had been much given to searching out the hollow places and recesses in the foundations of the castle, and who was often to be found with compass and ruler working away at a chart of the same which he had been in process of constructing, now came to the conclusion, that only by ascending the upper regions of his abode, could he become capable of understanding what lay beneath; and that, in all probability, one clear prospect, from the top of the highest attainable turret, over the castle as it lay below, would reveal more of the idea of its internal construction, that a year spent in wandering through its subterranean vaults. But the fact was, that the desire to ascend wakening within him had made him forget what was beneath; and having laid aside his chart for a time at least, he was now to be met in every quarter of the upper parts, searching and striving upward, now in one direction, now in another; and seeking, as he went, the best outlooks into the clear air of outer realities.

And they began to discover that they were all meditating different aspects of the same thing; and they brought together their various discoveries, and recognized the likeness between them; and the one thing often explained the other, and combining with it helped to a third. They grew in consequence more and more friendly and loving; so that every now and then, one turned to another and said, as in surprise, "Why, you are my brother!"—"Why, you are my sister!" And yet they had always known it.

The change reached to all. One, who lived on

the air of sweet sounds, and who was almost always to be found seated by her harp or some other instrument, had, till the late storm, been generally merry and playful, though sometimes sad. But for a long time after that, she was often found weeping, and playing little simple airs which she had heard in childhood—backward longings, followed by fresh tears. Before long, however, a new element manifested itself in her music. It became yet more wild, and sometimes retained all its sadness, but it was mingled with anticipation and hope. The past and the future merged in one ; and while memory yet brought the rain-cloud, expectation threw the rainbow across its bosom—and all was uttered in her music, which rose and swelled, now to defiance, now to victory; then died in a torrent of weeping.

As to the eldest sister, it was many days before

she recovered from the shock. At length, one day, her brother came to her, took her by the hand, led her to an open window, and told her to seat herself by it, and look out. She did so; but at first saw nothing more than an unsympathizing blaze of sunlight. But as she looked, the horizon widened out, and the dome of the sky ascended, till the grandeur seized upon her soul, and she fell on her knees and wept. Now the heavens seemed to bend lovingly over her, and to stretch out wide cloud-arms to embrace her; the earth lay like the bosom of an infinite love beneath her, and the wind kissed her cheek with an odour of roses. She sprang to her feet, and turned, in an agony of hope, expecting to behold the face of the father, but there stood only her brother, looking calmly though lovingly on her emotion. She turned again to the window. On the hill-tops rested the sky : Heaven and Earth were one ; and the prophecy awoke in her soul, that from betwixt them would the steps of the father approach.

Hitherto she had seen but Beauty; now she beheld truth. Often had she looked on such clouds as these, and loved the strange etherial curves into which the winds moulded them; and had smiled as her little pet sister told her what curious animals she saw in them, and tried to point them out to her. Now they were as troops of angels, jubilant over her new birth, for they sang, in her soul, of beauty, and truth, and love. She looked down, and her little sister knelt beside her.

She was a curious child, with black, glittering eyes, and dark hair; at the mercy of every wandering wind; a frolicsome, daring girl, who laughed more than she smiled. She was generally in attendance on her sister, and was always finding and bringing her strange things. She never pulled a primrose, but she knew the haunts of all the orchis tribe, and brought from them bees and butterflies innumerable, as offerings to her sister. Curious moths and glow-worms were her greatest delight; and she loved the stars, because they were like the glow-worms. But the change had affected her too; for her sister saw that her eyes had lost their glittering look, and had become more liquid and transparent. And from that time she often observed that her gaiety was more gentle, her smile more frequent, her laugh less bell-like; and although she was as wild as ever, there was more elegance in her motions, and more music in her voice. And she clung to her sister with far greater fondness than before.

The land reposed in the embrace of the warm summer days. The clouds of heaven nestled around the towers of the castle; and the hearts of its inmates became conscious of a warm atmosphere—of a presence of love. They began to feel like the children of a household, when the mother is at home. Their faces and forms grew daily more and more beautiful, till they wondered as they gazed on each other. As they walked in the gardens of the castle, or in the country around, they were often visited, especially the eldest sister, by sounds that no one heard but themselves, issuing from woods and waters; and by forms of love that lightened out of flowers, and grass, and great rocks. Now and then the young children would come in with a slow, stately step, and, with great eyes that looked as if they would devour all the creation, say that they had met the father amongst the trees, and that he had kissed them; "And," added one of them once, "I grew so big!" But when others went out to look, they could see no one. And some said it must have been the brother, who grew more and more beautiful, and loving, and reverend, and who had lost all traces of hardness, so that they wondered they could ever have thought him stern and harsh. But the eldest sister held her peace, and looked up, and her eyes filled with tears. " Who can tell," thought she, " but the little children know more about it than we ? "

Often, at sunrise, might be heard their hymn of praise to their unseen father, whom they felt to be near, though they saw him not. Some words thereof once reached my ear through the folds of the music in which they floated, as in an upward snow-storm of sweet sounds. And these are some of the words I heard—but there was much I seemed to hear, which I could not understand, and some things which I understood but cannot utter again.

" We thank thee that we have a father, and not a maker; that thou hast begotten us, and not moulded us as images of clay ; that we have come forth of thy heart, and have not been fashioned by thy hands. It *must* be so. Only the heart of a father is able to create. We rejoice in it, and bless thee that we know it. We thank thee for thyself. Be what thou art—our root and life, our beginning and end, our all in all. Come home to us. Thou livest; therefore we live. In thy light we see. Thou art—that is all our song."

Thus they worship, and love, and wait. Their hope and expectation grow ever stronger and brighter, that one day, ere long, the Father will show himself amongst them, and thenceforth dwell in his own house for evermore. What was once but an old legend has become the one desire of their hearts.

And the loftiest hope is the surest of being fulfilled.

THE WOW O' RIVVEN.

THE WOW O' RIVVEN.

ELSIE SCOTT had let her work fall on her knees, and her hands on her work, and was looking out of the wide, low window of her room, which was on one of the ground floors of the village street. Through a gap in the household shrubbery of fuchsias and myrtles filling the window-sill, one passing on the foot-pavement might get a momentary glimpse of her pale face, lighted up with two blue eyes, over which some inward trouble had spread a faint, gauze-like haziness. But almost before her thoughts had had time to wander back to this trouble, a shout of children's voices, at the other end of the street, reached her ear. She listened a moment. A shadow of displeasure and pain crossed her countenance; and rising hastily, she betook herself to an inner apartment, and closed the door behind her.

Meantime the sounds drew nearer; and by and by, an old man, whose strange appearance and dress showed that he had little capacity either for good or evil, passed the window. His clothes were comfortable enough in quality and condition, for they were the annual gift of a benevolent lady in the neighbourhood; but, being made to accommodate his taste, both known and traditional, they were somewhat peculiar in cut and adornment. Both coat and trousers were of a dark grey cloth; but the former, which, in its shape, partook of the military, had a straight collar of yellow, and narrow cuffs of the same; while upon both sleeves, about the place where a corporal wears his stripes, was expressed, in the same yellow cloth, a somewhat singular device. It was as close an imitation of a bell, with its tongue hanging out of its mouth, as the tailor's skill could produce from a single piece of cloth. The origin of the military cut of his coat was well known. His preference for it arose in the time of the wars of the first Napoleon, when the threatened invasion of the country caused the organization of many volunteer regiments. The martial show and exercises captivated the poor man's fancy; and from that time forward nothing pleased his vanity, and consequently conciliated his good-will more, than to style him by his favourite title—the *Colonel*. But the badge on his arm had a deeper origin, which will be partially manifest in the course of the story—if story it can be called. It was, indeed, the baptism of the fool, the outward and visible sign of his relation to the infinite and unseen. His countenance, however, although the features were not of any peculiarly low or animal type, showed no corresponding sign of the consciousness of such a relation, being as vacant as human countenance could well be.

The cause of Elsie's annoyance was that the fool was annoyed; he was followed by a troop of boys, who turned his rank into scorn, and assailed him with epithets hateful to him. Although the most harmless of creatures when let alone, he was dangerous when roused; and now he stooped repeatedly to pick up stones and hurl them at his tormentors, who took care, while abusing him, to keep at a considerable distance, lest he should get hold of them. Amidst the sounds of derision that followed him, might be heard the words frequently repeated—" *Come hâme, come hame.*" But in a few minutes the noise ceased, either from the interference of some friendly inhabitant, or that the boys grew weary, and departed in search of other amusement. By and by, Elsie might be seen again at her work in the window; but the cloud over her eyes was deeper, and her whole face more sad.

Indeed, so much did the persecution of this poor man affect her, that an onlooker would have been compelled to seek the cause in some yet deeper sympathy than that commonly felt for the oppressed, even by women. And such a sympathy existed, strange as it may seem, between the beautiful girl (for many called her *a bonnie lassie*) and this "tatter of humanity." Nothing would have been further from the thoughts of those that knew them, than the supposition of any correspondence or connexion between them; yet this sympathy sprang in part from a real similarity in their history and present condition.

All the facts that were known about *Feel Jock's* origin were these: that seventy years ago, a man who had gone with his horse and cart some miles from the village, to fetch home a load of peat from a desolate *moss*, had heard, while toiling along as rough a road on as lonely a hill-side as any in Scotland, the cry of a child; and, searching about, had found the infant, hardly wrapt in rags, and untended, as if the earth herself had just given him birth,—that desert moor, wide and dismal, broken and watery, the only bosom for him to lie upon, and the cold, clear night-heaven his only covering. The man had brought him home, and the parish had taken parish-care of him. He had grown up, and proved what he now was—almost an idiot. Many of the towns-people were kind to him, and employed him in fetching water for them from the river or wells in the neighbourhood, paying him for his trouble in victuals, or whisky, of which he was very fond. He seldom spoke; and the sentences he could utter were few; yet the tone, and even the words of his limited vocabulary, were sufficient to express gratitude and some measure of love towards those who were kind to him, and hatred of those who teased and insulted him. He lived a life without aim, and apparently to no purpose; in this resembling most of his more gifted fellow-men, who, with all the tools and materials necessary for building a noble mansion, are yet content with a clay hut.

Elsie, on the contrary, had been born in a comfortable farm-house, amidst homeliness and abundance. But at a very early age, she had lost both father and mother; not so early, however, but that she had faint memories of warm soft times on her mother's bosom, and of refuge in her mother's arms from the attacks of geese, and the pursuit of pigs. Therefore, in after-times, when she looked forward to heaven, it was as much a reverting to the old heavenly times of childhood and mother's love, as an anticipation of something yet to be revealed. Indeed, without some such memory, how should we ever picture to ourselves a perfect rest? But sometimes it would seem as if the more a heart was made capable of loving, the less it had to love; and poor Elsie, in passing from a mother's to a brother's guardianship, felt a change of spiritual temperature too keen. He was not a bad man, or incapable of benevolence when touched by the sight of want in anything of which he would himself have felt the privation; but he was so coarsely made, that only the purest animal necessities affected him; and a hard word, or unfeeling speech, could never have reached the quick of his nature through the hide that enclosed it. Elsie, on the contrary, was excessively and painfully sensitive, as if her nature constantly protended an invisible multitude of half-spiritual, half-nervous antennæ, which shrank and trembled in every current of air at all below their own temperature. The effect of this upon her behaviour was such, that she was called odd; and the poor girl felt she was not like other people, yet could not help it. Her brother, too, laughed at her without the slightest idea of the pain he occasioned, or the remotest feeling of curiosity as to what the inward and consistent causes of the outward abnormal condition might be. Tenderness was the divine comforting she needed; and it was altogether absent from her brother's character and behaviour.

Her neighbours looked on her with some interest, but they rather shunned than courted her acquaintance; especially after the return of certain nervous attacks, to which she had been subject in childhood, and which were again brought on by the events I must relate. It is curious how certain diseases repel, by a kind of awe, the sympathies of the neighbours: as if, by the fact of being subject to them, the patient were removed into another realm of existence, from which, like the dead with the living, she can hold communion with those around her only partially, and with a mixture of dread pervading the inter-course. Thus some of the deepest, purest wells of spiritual life, are, like those in old castles, choked up by the decay of the outer walls. But what tended more than anything, perhaps, to keep up the painful unrest of her soul (for the beauty of her character was evident in the fact, that the irritation seldom reached her *mind*), was a cir-cumstance at which, in its present connexion, some of my readers will smile, and others feel a shudder corresponding in kind to that of Elsie.

Her brother was very fond of a rather small, but ferocious-looking bull-dog, which followed close at his heels, wherever he went, with hanging head and slouching gait, never leaping or racing about like other dogs. When in the house, he always lay under his master's chair. He seemed to dislike Elsie, and she felt an unspeakable repugnance to him. Though she never mentioned her aversion, her brother easily saw it by the way in which she avoided the animal; and attributing it entirely to fear—which indeed had a great share in the matter—he would cruelly aggravate it, by telling her stories of the fierce hardihood and relentless persistency of this kind of animal. He dared not yet further increase her terror by offering to set the creature upon her, because it was doubtful whether he might be able to restrain him; but the mental suffering which he occasioned by this heartless conduct, and for which he had no

sympathy, was as severe as many bodily sufferings
to which he would have been sorry to subject her.
Whenever the poor girl happened inadvertently to
pass near the dog, which was seldom, a low growl
made her aware of his proximity, and drove her to
a quick retreat. He was, in fact, the animal
impersonation of the animal opposition which she
had continually to endure. Like chooses like ;
and the bull-dog *in* her brother made choice of
the bull-dog *out of* him for his companion. So
her day was one of shrinking fear and multiform
discomfort.

But a nature capable of so much distress, must
of necessity be *capable* of a corresponding amount
of pleasure ; and in her case this was manifest in
the fact, that sleep and the quiet of her own room
restored her wonderfully. If she was only let
alone, a calm mood, filled with images of pleasure,
soon took possession of her mind.

Her acquaintance with the fool had commenced some ten years previous to the time I write of, when she was quite a little girl, and had come from the country with her brother, who, having taken a small farm close to the town, preferred residing in the town to occupying the farm-house, which was not comfortable. She looked at first with some terror on his uncouth appearance, and with much wonderment on his strange dress. This wonder was heightened by a conversation she overheard one day in the street, between the fool and a little pale-faced boy, who, approaching him respectfully, said, "Weel, cornel!" "Weel, laddie!" was the reply. "Fat dis the wow say, cornel?" "Come hame, come hame!" answered the *colonel*, with both accent and quantity heaped on the word *hame*. . What the *wow* could be, she had no idea; only, as the years passed on, the strange word became in her mind indescribably associated with the strange shape in yellow cloth on his sleeves. Had she been a native of the town, she could not have failed to know its import, so familiar was every one with it, although it did not belong to the local vocabulary ; but, as it was, years passed away before she discovered its meaning. And when, again and again, the fool, attempting to convey his gratitude for some kindness she had shown him, mumbled over the words—" *The wow o' Rivven—the wow o' Rivven,*" the wonder would return as to what could be the idea associated with them in his mind, but she made no advance towards their explanation.

That, however, which most attracted her to the old man, was his persecution by the children. They were to him what the bull-dog was to her— the constant source of irritation and annoyance. They could hardly hurt him, nor did he appear to dread other injury from them than insult, to which, fool though he was, he was keenly alive. Human gad-flies that they were! they sometimes stung him beyond endurance, and he would curse them in the impotence of his anger. Once or twice Elsie had been so far carried beyond her constitutional timidity, by sympathy for the distress of her friend, that she had gone out and talked to the boys,—even scolded them, so that they slunk away ashamed, and began to stand as much in dread of her as of the clutches of their prey. So she, gentle and timid to excess, acquired among them the reputation of a termagant. Popular opinion among children, as among men, is often just, but as often very unjust; for the same manifestations may proceed from opposite principles; and, therefore, as indices to character, may mislead as often as enlighten.

Next door to the house in which Elsie resided, dwelt a tradesman and his wife, who kept an indefinite sort of shop, in which various kinds of goods were exposed for sale. Their youngest son was about the same age as Elsie; and while they were rather more than children, and less than young people, he spent many of his evenings with her, somewhat to the loss of position in his classes at the parish school. They were, indeed, much attached to each other; and, peculiarly constituted as Elsie was, one may imagine what kind of heavenly messenger a companion stronger than herself must have been to her. In fact, if she could have framed the undefinable need of her child-like nature into an articulate prayer, it would have been—"Give me some one to love me stronger than I." Any love was helpful, yes, in its degree, saving to her poor troubled soul; but the hope, as they grew older together, that the powerful, yet tender-hearted youth, really loved her, and would one day make her his wife, was like the opening of heavenly eyes of life and love in the hitherto blank and death-like face of her existence.   But nothing had been said of love, although they met and parted like lovers.

Doubtless, if the circles of their thought and feeling had continued as now to intersect each other, there would have been no interruption to their affection; but the time at length arrived when the old couple, seeing the rest of their family comfortably settled in life, resolved to make a gentleman of the youngest; and so sent him from school to college. The facilities existing in Scotland for providing a professional training enabled them to educate him as a surgeon. He parted from Elsie with some regret; but, far less dependent on her than she was on him, and full of the prospects of the future, he felt none of that sinking at the heart which seemed to lay her whole nature open to a fresh inroad of all the terrors and sorrows of her peculiar existence. No correspondence took place between them. New pursuits and relations, and the development of his tastes and judgments, entirely altered the position of poor Elsie in his memory. Having been, during their intercourse, far less of a man than she of a woman, he had no definite idea of the place he had occupied in her regard; and in his mind she receded into the background of the past, without his having any idea that she would suffer thereby, or that he was unjust towards her; while, in her thoughts, his image stood in the highest and clearest relief. It was the centre-point from which and towards which all lines radiated and converged; and although she could not but be doubtful about the future, yet there was much hope mingled with her doubts.

But when, at the close of two years, he visited his native village, and she saw before her, instead of the homely youth who had left her that winter evening, one who, to her inexperienced eyes, appeared a finished gentleman, her heart sank within her, as if she had found Nature herself false in her ripening processes, destroying the beautiful promise of a former year by changing instead of developing her creations. He spoke kindly to her, but not cordially. To her ear the voice seemed to 'come from a great distance out of the past; and while she looked upon him, that optical change passed over her vision, which all have experienced after gazing abstractedly on any object for a time: his form grew very small, and receded to an immeasurable distance; till, her imagination mingling with the twilight haze of her senses, she seemed to see him standing far off on a hill, with the bright horizon of sunset for a background to his clearly defined figure.

She knew no more till she found herself in bed

in the dark; and the first message that reached her from the outer world, was the infernal growl of the bull-dog from the room below. Next day she saw her lover walking with two ladies, who would have thought it some degree of condescension to speak to her; and he passed the house without once looking towards it.

One who is sufficiently possessed by the demon of nervousness to be glad of the magnetic influences of a friend's company in a public promenade, or of a horse beneath him in passing through a churchyard, will have some faint idea of how utterly exposed and defenceless poor Elsie now felt on the crowded thoroughfare of life. And so the insensibility which had overtaken her, was not the ordinary swoon with which Nature relieves the overstrained nerves, but the return of the epileptic fits of her early childhood; and if the condition of the poor girl had been pitiable before, it was tenfold more so now. Yet she did not complain, but bore all in silence, though it was evident that her health was giving way. But now, help came to her from a strange quarter; though many might not be willing to accord the name of help to that which rather hastened than retarded the progress of her decline.

She had gone to spend a few of the summer days with a relative in the country, some miles from her home, if home it could be called. One evening, towards sunset, she went out for a solitary walk. Passing from the little garden-gate, she went along a bare country road for some distance, and then, turning aside by a footpath through a thicket of low trees, she came out in a lonely little churchyard on the hill-side. Hardly knowing whether or not she had intended to go there, she seated herself on a mound covered with long grass, one of many. Before her stood the ruins of an old church which was taking centuries to crumble. Little remained but the gable-wall, immensely thick, and covered with ancient ivy. The rays of the setting sun fell on a mound at its foot, not green like the rest, but of a rich, red-brown in the rosy sunset, and evidently but newly heaped up. Her eyes, too, rested upon it. Slowly the sun sank below the near horizon.

As the last brilliant point disappeared, the ivy darkened, and a wind arose and shook all its leaves, making them look cold and troubled; and to Elsie's ear came a low faint sound, as from a far-off bell. But close beside her—and she started and shivered at the sound—rose a deep, mono-tonous, almost sepulchral voice, *"Come hame, come hame! The wow, the wow!"*

At once she understood the whole. She sat in the churchyard of the ancient parish church of Ruthven; and when she lifted up her eyes, there she saw, in the half-ruined belfry, the old bell, all but hidden with ivy, which the passing wind had roused to utter one sleepy tone; and there, beside her, stood the fool with the bell on his arm; and to him and to her the *wow o' Rivven* said, "*Come hame, come hame!*" Ah, what did she want in the whole universe of God but a home? And though the ground beneath was hard, and the sky overhead far and boundless, and the hill-side lonely and companionless, yet somewhere within the visible, and beyond these the outer surfaces of creation, there might be a home for her; as round the wintry house the snows lie heaped up cold and white and dreary all the long *forenight*, while within, beyond the closed shutters, and giving no glimmer through the thick stone walls, the fires are blazing joyously, and the voices and laughter of young unfrozen children are heard, and nothing belongs to winter but the grey hairs on the heads of the parents, within whose warm hearts child-like voices are heard, and child-like thoughts move to and fro. The kernel of winter itself is spring, or a sleeping summer.

It was no wonder that the fool, cast out of the earth on a far more desolate spot than this, should seek to return within her bosom at this place of open doors, and should call it *home.* For surely the surface of the earth had no home for him. The mound at the foot of the gable contained the body of one who had shown him kindness. He had followed the funeral that afternoon from the town, and had remained behind with the bell. Indeed, it was his custom, though Elsie had not known it, to follow every funeral going to this, his favourite churchyard of Ruthven; and, possibly in imitation of its booming, for it was still tolled at the funerals, he had given the old bell the name of *the wow,* and had translated its monotonous clangour into the articulate sounds—*come hame, come hame.* What precise meaning he attached to the words, it is impossible to say; but it was evident that the place possessed a strange attraction for him, drawing him towards it by the cords of some spiritual magnetism. It is possible that in the mind of the idiot there may have been some feeling about this churchyard and bell, which, in the mind of another, would have become a grand poetic thought; a feeling as if the ghostly old bell hung at the church-door of the invisible world, and ever and anon rung out joyous notes (though they sounded sad in the ears of the living), calling to the children of the unseen to *come home, come home.* She sat for some time in silence; for the bell did not ring again, and the fool spoke no more; till the dews began to fall, when she rose and went home, followed by her companion, who passed the night in the barn.

From that hour Elsie was furnished with a visual image of the rest she sought; an image which, mingling with deeper and holier thoughts, became, like the bow set in the cloud, the earthly pledge and sign of the fulfilment of heavenly hopes. Often when the wintry fog of cold discomfort and homelessness filled her soul, all at once the picture of the little churchyard—with the old gable and belfry, and the slanting sunlight steeping down to the very roots of the long grass on the graves—arose in the darkened chamber (*camera obscura*) of her soul; and again she heard the faint Æolian sound of the bell, and the voice of the prophet-fool who interpreted the oracle; and the inward weariness was soothed by the promise of a long sleep. Who can tell how many have been counted fools simply because they were prophets; or how much of the madness in the world may be the utterance of thoughts true and just, but belonging to a region differing from ours in its nature and scenery!

But to Elsie looking out of her window came the mocking tones of the idle boys who had chosen as the vehicle of their scorn the very words which showed the relation of the fool to the eternal, and revealed in him an element higher far than any yet developed in them. They turned his glory into shame, like the enemies of David when they mocked the would-be king. And the best in a man is often that which is most condemned by those who have not attained to his goodness. The words, however, even as repeated by the boys, had not solely awakened indignation at the persecution of the old man: they had likewise comforted her with the thought of the refuge that awaited both him and her.

But the same evening a worse trial was in store for her. Again she sat near the window, oppressed by the consciousness that her brother had come in. He had gone up-stairs, and his dog had remained at the door, exchanging surly compliments with some of his own kind, when the fool came strolling past, and, I do not know from what cause, the dog flew at him. Elsie heard his cry and looked up. Her fear of the brute vanished in a moment before her sympathy for her friend. She darted from the house, and rushed towards the dog to drag him off the defenceless idiot, calling him by his name in a tone of anger and dislike. He left the fool, and, springing at Elsie, seized her by the arm above the elbow with such a gripe that, in the midst of her agony, she fancied she heard the bone crack. But she uttered no cry, for the most apprehensive are sometimes the most courageous. Just then, however, her former lover was coming along the street, and, catching a glimpse of what had happened, was on the spot in an instant, took the dog by the throat with a gripe not inferior to his own, and having thus compelled him to relax his hold, dashed him on the ground with a force that almost stunned him, and then with a superadded kick sent him away limping and howling; whereupon the fool, attacking him furiously with a stick, would certainly have finished him, had not his master descried his plight and come to his rescue.

Meantime the young surgeon had carried Elsie into the house; for, as soon as she was rescued from the dog, she had fallen down in one of her fits, which were becoming more and more frequent of themselves, and little needed such a shock as this to increase their violence. He was dressing her arm when she began to recover; and when she opened her eyes, in a state of half-consciousness, the first object she beheld, was his face bending over her. Recalling nothing of what had occurred, it seemed to her, in the dreamy condition in which the fit had left her, the same face, unchanged, which had once shone in upon her tardy spring-time, and promised to ripen it into summer. She forgot it had departed and left her in the wintry cold. And so she uttered wild words of love and trust; and the youth, while stung with remorse at his own neglect, was astonished to perceive the poetic forms of beauty in which the soul of the uneducated maiden burst into flower. But as her senses recovered themselves, the face gradually changed to her, as if the slow alteration of two years had been phantasmagorically compressed into a few moments; and the glow departed from the maiden's thoughts and words, and her soul found itself at the narrow window of the present, from which she could behold but a dreary country.—From the street came the iambic cry of the fool, " Come hame, come hame."

Tycho Brahe, I think, is said to have kept a fool, who frequently sat at his feet in his study, and to whose mutterings he used to listen in the pauses of his own thought. The shining soul of the astronomer drew forth the rainbow of harmony from the misty spray of words ascending ever from the dark gulf into which the thoughts of the idiot were ever falling. He beheld curious concurrences of words therein, and could read strange meanings from them—sometimes even received wondrous hints for the direction of celestial inquiry, from what, to any other, and it may be to the fool himself, was but a ceaseless and aimless babble. Such power lieth in words. It is not then to be wondered at, that the sounds I have mentioned should fall on the ears of Elsie, at such a moment, as a message from God himself.

This then—all this dreariness—was but a passing show like the rest, and there lay somewhere for her a reality—a home. The tears burst up from her oppressed heart. She received the message, and prepared to go home. From that time her strength gradually sank, but her spirits as steadily rose.

The strength of the fool, too, began to fail, for he was old. He bore all the signs of age, even to the grey hairs, which betokened no wisdom. But one cannot say what wisdom might be in him, or how far he had not fought his own battle, and been victorious. Whether any notion of a continuance of life and thought dwelt in his brain, it is impossible to tell; but he seemed to have the idea that this was not his home; and those who saw him gradually approaching his end, might well anticipate for him a higher life in the world to come. He had passed through this world without ever awaking to such a consciousness of being as is common to mankind. He had spent his years like a weary dream through a long night,—a strange, dismal, unkindly dream; and now the morning was at hand. Often in his dream had he listened with sleepy senses to the ringing of the bell, but that bell would awake him at last. He was like a seed buried too deep in the soil, to which the light has never penetrated, and which, therefore, has never forced its way upwards to the open air, never experienced the resurrection of the dead. But seeds will grow ages after they have fallen into the earth; and, indeed, with many kinds, and within some limits, the older the seed before it germinates, the more plentiful the fruit. And may it not be believed of many human beings, that, the great Husbandman having sown them like seeds in the soil of human affairs, there they lie buried a life long; and only after the upturning of the soil by death, reach a position in which the awakening of their aspiration and the consequent growth become possible. Surely he has made nothing in vain.

A violent cold and cough brought him at last near to his end, and hearing that he was ill, Elsie ventured one bright spring day to go to see him. When she entered the miserable room where he lay, he held out his hand to her with something like a smile, and muttered feebly and painfully, "I'm gaein' to the wow, nae to come back again." Elsie could not restrain her tears ; while the old man, looking fixedly at her, though with meaningless eyes, muttered, for the last time, "*Come hame! come hame!*" and sank into a lethargy, from which nothing could rouse him, till, next morning, he was waked by friendly death from the long sleep of this world's night. They bore him to his favourite churchyard, and buried him within the site of the old church, below his loved bell, which had ever been to him as the cuckoo-note of a coming spring.   Thus he at length obeyed its summons, and went home.

Elsie lingered till the first summer days lay warm on the land.   Several kind hearts in the village, hearing of her illness, visited her and ministered to her.   Wondering at her sweetness and patience, they regretted they had not known her before.   How much consolation might not their kindness have imparted, and how much might not their sympathy have strengthened her on her painful road!   But they could not long have delayed her going home.   Nor, mentally consti-tuted as she was, would this have been at all to be desired.   Indeed it was chiefly the expectation of departure that quieted and soothed her tremulous nature.   It is true that a deep spring of hope and faith kept singing on in her heart, but this alone, without the anticipation of speedy release, could only have kept her mind at peace. It could not have reached, at least for a long time, the border land between body and mind, in which her disease lay.

One still night of summer, the nurse who watched by her bed-side heard her murmur through her sleep, "I hear it : *come hame—come hame.* I'm comin', I'm comin'—I'm gaein' hame to the wow, nae to come back." She awoke at the sound of her own words, and begged the nurse to convey to her brother her last request, that she might be buried by the side of the fool, within the old church of Ruthven. Then she turned her face to the wall, and in the morning was found quiet and cold. She must have died within a few minutes after her last words. She was buried according to her request ; and thus she too went home.

Side by side rest the aged fool and the young,

maiden; for the bell called them, and they obeyed; and surely they found the fire burning bright, and heard friendly voices, and felt sweet lips on theirs, in the home to which they went. Surely both intellect and love were waiting them there.

Still the old bell hangs in the old gable; and whenever another is borne to the old churchyard, it keeps calling to those who are left behind, with the same sad, but friendly and unchanging voice—

" Come hame ! come hame ! come hame ! "

"Thy sun shall no more go down; neither shall thy moon withdraw itself: for the LORD shall be thine everlasting light, and the days of thy mourning shall be ended."—*Isaiah* lx. 20.

THE BROKEN SWORDS.

THE BROKEN SWORDS.

HE eyes of three, two sisters and a brother, gazed for the last time on a great pale-golden star, that followed the sun down the steep west. It went down to arise again; and the brother about to depart might return, but more than the usual doubt hung upon his future. For between the white dresses of the sisters, shone his scarlet coat and golden sword-knot, which he had put on for the first time, more to gratify their pride than his own vanity. The brightening moon, as if prophetic of a future memory, had already begun to dim the scarlet and the gold, and to give them a pale, ghostly hue. In her thoughtful light the whole group seemed more like a meeting in the land of shadows, than a parting in the substantial earth.— But which should be called the land of realities?—the region where appearance, and space, and time drive between, and stop the flowing currents of the soul's speech? or that region where heart meets heart, and appearance has become the slave to utterance, and space and time are forgotten?

Through the quiet air came the far-off rush of water, and the near cry of the land-rail. Now and then a chilly wind blew unheeded through the startled and jostling leaves that shaded the ivy-seat. Else, there was calm everywhere, rendered yet deeper and more intense by the dusky sorrow that filled their hearts. For, far away, hundreds of miles beyond the hearing of their ears, roared the great war-guns; next week their brother must sail with his regiment to join the army ; and to-morrow he must leave his home.

The sisters looked on him tenderly, with vague fears about his fate. Yet little they divined it. That the face they loved might lie pale and bloody, in a heap of slain, was the worst image of it that arose before them ; but this, had they seen the future, they would, in ignorance of the further future, have infinitely preferred to that which awaited him. And even while they looked on him, a dim feeling of the unsuitableness of his lot filled their minds. For, indeed, to all judgments it must have seemed unsuitable that the home-boy, the loved of his mother, the pet of his sisters, who was happy, womanlike, (as Coleridge says,) if he possessed the signs of love, having never yet sought for its proofs—that he should be sent amongst soldiers, to command and be com-manded ; to kill, or perhaps to be himself crushed out of the fair earth in the uproar that brings back for the moment the reign of Night and Chaos. No wonder that to his sisters it seemed strange and sad. Yet such was their own position in the battle of life, in which their father had died with doubtful conquest, that when their old military uncle sent the boy an ensign's commission, they did not dream of refusing the only path open, as they thought, to an honourable profession, even though it might lead to the trench-grave. They heard it as the voice of destiny, wept, and yielded.

If they had possessed a deeper insight into his character, they would have discovered yet further reason to doubt the fitness of the profession chosen for him ; and if they had ever seen him at school, it is possible the doubt of fitness might have strengthened into a certainty of incongruity. His comparative inactivity amongst his school-fellows, though occasioned by no dulness of intellect, might have suggested the necessity of a quiet life, if inclination and liking had been the arbiters in the choice. Nor was this inactivity the result of defective animal spirits either, for sometimes his mirth and boyish frolic were unbounded ; but it seemed to proceed from an over-activity of the inward life, absorbing, and in some measure checking, the outward manifestation. He had so much to do in his own hidden kingdom, that he had not time to take his place in the polity and strife of the commonwealth around him. Hence, while other boys were acting, he was thinking. In this point of difference, he felt keenly the superiority of many of his companions ; for another boy would have the obstacle overcome, or the adversary subdued, while he was meditating on the propriety, or on the means, of effecting the desired end. He envied their promptitude, while they never saw reason to envy his wisdom; for his conscience, tender and not strong, frequently transformed slowness of determination into irre-solution ; while a delicacy of the sympathetic nerves tended to distract him from any pre-determined course, by the diversity of their vibrations, responsive to influences from all quarters, and destructive to unity of purpose.

Of such a one, the *à priori* judgment would be, that he ought to be left to meditate and grow for some time, before being called upon to produce the fruits of action. But add to these mental conditions a vivid imagination, and a high sense of honour, nourished in childhood by the reading of the old knightly romances, and then put the youth in a position in which action is imperative, and you have elements of strife sufficient to reduce that fair kingdom of his, to utter anarchy and madness. Yet so little do we know ourselves, and so different are the symbols with which the imagination works its algebra, from the realities which those symbols represent, that as yet the youth felt no uneasiness, but contemplated his new calling with a glad enthusiasm and some vanity; for all his prospect lay in the glow of the scarlet and the gold. Nor did this excitement receive any check till the day before his departure, on which day I have introduced him to my readers, when, accidentally taking up a newspaper of a week old, his eye fell on these words—"*Already crying women are to be met in the streets.*" With this cloud afar on his horizon, which, though no bigger than a man's hand, yet cast a perceptible shadow over his mind, he departed next morning. The coach carried him beyond the consecrated circle of home-laws and impulses, out into the great tumult, above which rises ever and anon the cry of Cain, "Am I my brother's keeper?"

Every tragedy of higher order, constructed in

Christian times, will correspond more or less to the grand drama of the Bible ; wherein the first act opens with a brilliant sunset vision of Paradise, in which childish sense and need are served with all the profusion of the indulgent nurse.   But the glory fades off into grey and black, and night settles down upon the heart which, rightly uncontent with the childish, and not having yet learned the childlike, seeks knowledge and manhood as a thing denied by the Maker, and yet to be gained by the creature ; so sets forth alone to climb the heavens, and instead of climbing, falls into the abyss.   Then follows the long dismal night of feverish efforts and delirious visions, or, it may be, helpless despair; till at length a deeper stratum of the soul is heaved to the surface ; and amid the first dawn of morning, the youth says within him, " I have sinned against my *Maker*—I will arise and go to my *Father*."   More or less, I say, will

Christian tragedy correspond to this—a fall and a rising again ; not a rising only, but a victory ; not a victory merely, but a triumph. Such, in its way and degree, is my story. I have shown, in one passing scene, the home-paradise ; now I have to show a scene of a far differing nature.

The young ensign was lying in his tent, weary, but wakeful. All day long the cannon had been bellowing against the walls of the city, which now lay with wide, gaping breach, ready for the morrow's storm, but covered yet with the friendly darkness. His regiment was ordered to be ready with the earliest dawn to march up to the breach. That day, for the first time, there had been blood on his sword—there the sword lay, a spot on the chased hilt still. He had cut down one of the enemy in a skirmish with a sallying party of the besieged, and the look of the man as he fell, haunted him. He felt, for the time, that he dared not pray to the Father, for the blood of a brother had rushed forth at the stroke of his arm, and there was one fewer of living souls on the earth because he lived thereon. And to-morrow he must lead a troop of men up to that poor disabled town, and turn them loose upon it, not knowing what might follow in the triumph of enraged and victorious foes, who for weeks had been subjected, by the constancy of the place, to the greatest privations. It was true the general had issued his commands against all disorder and pillage; but if the soldiers once yielded to temptation, what might not be done before the officers could reclaim them! All the wretched tales he had read of the sack of cities, rushed back on his memory. He shuddered as he lay. Then his conscience began to speak, and to ask what right he had to be there.—Was the war a just one?—He could not tell; for this was a bad time for settling nice questions. But there he was, right or wrong, fighting and shedding blood on God's earth, beneath God's heaven.

Over and over he turned the question in his mind; again and again the spouting blood of his foe, and the death-look in his eye, rose before him; and the youth who at school could never fight with a companion because he was not sure that he was in the right, was alone in the midst of undoubting men of war, amongst whom he was driven helplessly along, upon the waves of a terrible necessity. What wonder that in the midst of these perplexities his courage should fail him! What wonder that the consciousness of fainting should increase the faintness! or that the dread of fear and its consequences should hasten and invigorate its attacks! To crown all, when he dropped into a troubled slumber at length, he found himself hurried, as on a storm of fire, through the streets of the captured town, from all the windows of which looked forth familiar faces, old and young, but distorted from the memory of his boyhood by fear and wild despair. On one spot lay the body of his father, with his face to the earth ; and he woke at the cry of horror and rage that burst from his own lips, as he saw the rough, bloody hand of a soldier twisted in the loose hair of his elder sister, and the younger fainting in the arms of a scoundrel belonging to his own regiment.

He slept no more. As the grey morning broke, the troops appointed for the attack assembled without sound of trumpet or drum, and were silently formed in fitting order. The young ensign was in his place, weary and wretched after his miserable night. Before him he saw a great, broad-shouldered lieutenant, whose brawny hand seemed almost too large for his sword-hilt, and in any one of whose limbs played more animal life than in the whole body of the pale youth. The firm-set lips of this officer, and the fire of his eye, showed a concentrated resolution, which, by the contrast, increased the misery of the ensign, and seemed, as if the stronger absorbed the weaker, to draw out from him the last fibres of self-possession : the sight of unattainable determination, while it increased the feeling of the arduousness of that which required such determination, threw him into the great gulf which lay between him and it. In this disorder of his nervous and mental condition, with a doubting conscience and a shrinking heart, is it any wonder that the terrors which lay before him at the gap in those bristling walls, should draw near, and making sudden inroad upon his soul, overwhelm the government of a will worn out by the tortures of an unassured spirit? What share fear contributed to unman him, it was impossible for him, in the dark, confused conflict of differing emotions, to determine ; but doubtless a natural shrinking from danger, there being no excitement to deaden its influence, and no hope of victory to encourage to the struggle, seeing victory was dreadful to him as defeat, had its part in the sad result. Many men who have courage, are dependent on ignorance and a low state of the moral feeling for that courage ; and a further progress towards the development of the higher nature would, for a time at least, entirely overthrow it. Nor could such loss of courage be rightly designated by the name of cowardice.

But, alas ! the colonel happened to fix his eyes upon him as he passed along the file ; and this completed his confusion. He betrayed such evident symptoms of perturbation, that that officer ordered him under arrest ; and the result was, that, chiefly for the sake of example to the army, he was, upon trial by court-martial, expelled from the service, and had his sword broken over his head. Alas for the delicate-minded youth! Alas for the home-darling!

Long after, he found at the bottom of his chest the pieces of the broken sword, and remembered that, at the time, he had lifted them from the ground and carried them away. But he could not recall under what impulse he had done so. Perhaps the agony he suffered, passing the bounds of mortal endurance, had opened for him a vista into the eternal, and had shown him, if not the injustice of the sentence passed upon him, yet his freedom from blame, or, endowing him with dim prophetic vision, had given him the assurance that some day the stain would be wiped from his soul, and leave him standing clear before the tribunal of his own honour. Some feeling like this, I say, may have caused him, with a passing gleam of indignant protest, to lift the fragments from the earth, and carry them away; even as the friends of a so-called traitor may bear away his mutilated body from the wheel. But if such was the case, the vision was soon overwhelmed and forgotten in the succeeding anguish. He could not see that, in mercy to his doubting spirit, the question which had agitated his mind almost to madness, and which no results of the impending conflict could have settled for him, was thus quietly set aside for the time; nor that, painful as was the dark, dreadful existence that he was now to pass in self-torment and moaning, it would go by, and leave his spirit clearer far, than if, in his apprehension, it had been stained with further blood-guiltiness, instead of the loss of honour. Years after, when he accidentally learned that on that very morning the whole of his company, with parts of several more, had, or ever they began to mount the breach, been blown to pieces by the explosion of a mine, he cried aloud in bitterness, "Would God that my fear had not been discovered before I reached that spot!" But surely it is better to pass into the next region of life having reaped some assurance, some firmness of character, determination of effort, and consciousness of the worth of life, in the present world; so approaching the future steadily and faithfully, and if in much darkness and ignorance, yet not in the oscillations of moral uncertainty.

Close upon the catastrophe followed a torpor, which lasted he did not know how long, and which wrapped in a thick fog all the succeeding events. For some time he can hardly be said to have had any conscious history. He awoke to life and torture when half way across the sea towards his native country, where was no home any longer for him. To this point, and no further, could his thoughts return in after years. But the misery which he then endured is hardly to be understood, save by those of like delicate temperament with himself. All day long he sat silent in his cabin; nor could any effort of the captain, or others on board, induce him to go on deck till night came on, when, under the starlight, he ventured into the open air. The sky soothed him then, he knew not how. For the face of nature is the face of God, and must bear expressions that can influence, though unconsciously to them, the most ignorant and hopeless of his children. Often did he watch the clouds in hope of a storm, his spirit rising and falling as the sky darkened or cleared; he longed, in the necessary selfishness of such suffering, for a tumult of waters to swallow the vessel; and only the recollection of how many lives were involved in its safety besides his own, prevented him from praying to God for lightning and tempest, borne on which he might dash into the haven of the other world. One night, following a sultry calm day, he thought that Mercy had heard his unuttered prayer. The air and sea were intense darkness, till a light as intense for one moment annihilated it, and the succeeding darkness seemed shattered with the sharp reports of the thunder that cracked without reverberation. He who had shrunk from battle with his fellow-men, rushed to the mainmast, threw himself on his knees, and stretched forth his arms in speechless energy of supplication; but the storm passed away overhead, and left him kneeling still by the uninjured mast. At length the vessel reached her port. He hurried on shore to bury himself in the most secret place he could find. *Out of sight* was his first, his only thought.

Return to his mother he would not, he could not; and, indeed, his friends never learned his fate, until it had carried him far beyond their reach.

For several weeks he lurked about like a male-factor, in low lodging-houses in narrow streets of the sea-port to which the vessel had borne him, heeding no one, and but little shocked at the strange society and conversation with which, though only in bodily presence, he had to mingle. These formed the subjects of reflection in after times; and he came to the conclusion that, though much evil and much misery exist, suffi-cient to move prayers and tears in those who love their kind, yet there is less of both than those looking down from a more elevated social position upon the weltering heap of humanity, are ready to imagine; especially if they regard it likewise from the pedestal of self-congratulation on which a meagre type of religion has elevated them. But at length his little stock of money was nearly expended, and there was nothing that he could do, or learn to do, in this sea-port. He felt impelled to seek manual labour, partly because he thought it more likely he could obtain that sort of employment, without a request for reference as to his character, which would lead to inquiry about his previous history; and partly, perhaps, from an instinctive feeling that hard bodily labour would tend to lessen his inward suffering.

He left the town, therefore, at night-fall of a July day, carrying a little bundle of linen, and the remains of his money, somewhat augmented by the sale of various articles of clothing and con-venience, which his change of life rendered super-fluous and unsuitable. He directed his course northwards, travelling principally by night—so painfully did he shrink from the gaze even of footfarers like himself; and sleeping during the day in some hidden nook of wood or thicket, or under the shadow of a great tree in a solitary field. So fine was the season, that for three successive weeks he was able to travel thus without inconvenience, lying down when the sun grew hot in the forenoon, and generally waking when the first faint stars were hesitating in the great darkening heavens that covered and shielded him. For above every cloud, above every storm, rise up, calm, clear, divine, the deep infinite skies; they embrace the tempest even as the sunshine; by their permission it exists within their boundless peace: therefore it cannot hurt, and must pass away, while there they stand as ever, domed up eternally, lasting, strong, and pure.

Several times he attempted to get agricultural employment; but the whiteness of his hands and

the tone of his voice not merely suggested unfit-
ness for labour, but generated suspicion as to the
character of one who had evidently dropped from
a rank so much higher, and was seeking admit-
tance within the natural masonic boundaries and
secrets and privileges of another. Disheartened
somewhat, but hopeful, he journeyed on. I say
hopeful; for the blessed power of life in the
universe, in fresh air and sunshine absorbed by
active exercise, in winds, yea in rain, though it
fell but seldom, had begun to work its natural
healing, soothing effect, upon his perturbed spirit.
And there was room for hope in his new en-
deavour. As his bodily strength increased, and
his health, considerably impaired by inward
suffering, improved, the trouble of his soul
became more endurable—and in some measure
to endure is to conquer and destroy. In proportion as the mind grows in the strength of patience,

the disturber of its peace sickens and fades away. At length, one day, a widow lady in a village through which his road led him, gave him a day's work in her garden. He laboured hard and well, notwithstanding his soon-blistered hands, received his wages thankfully, and found a resting-place for the night on the low part of a hay-stack from which the upper portion had been cut away. Here he ate his supper of bread and cheese, pleased to have found such comfortable quarters, and soon fell fast asleep.

When he awoke, the whole heavens and earth seemed to give a full denial to sin and sorrow. The sun was just mounting over the horizon, looking up the clear cloud-mottled sky. From millions of water-drops hanging on the bending stalks of grass, sparkled his rays in varied refraction, transformed here to a gorgeous burning ruby, there to an emerald, green as the grass, and yonder to a flashing, sunny topaz. The chanting priest-lark had gone up from the low earth, as soon as the heavenly light had begun to enwrap and illumine the folds of its tabernacle; and had entered the high heavens with his offering, whence, unseen, he now dropped on the earth the sprinkled sounds of his overflowing blessedness. The poor youth rose but to kneel, and cry, from a bursting heart, "Hast thou not, O Father, some care for me? Canst thou not restore my lost honour? Can anything befall thy children for which thou hast no help? Surely, if the face of thy world lie not, joy and not grief is at the heart of the universe. Is there none for me?"

The highest poetic feeling of which we are now conscious, springs not from the beholding of perfected beauty, but from the mute sympathy which the creation with all its children manifests with us in the groaning and travailing which look for the sonship. Because of our need and aspiration, the snowdrop gives birth in our hearts to a loftier spiritual and poetic feeling, than the rose most complete in form, colour, and odour. The rose is of Paradise—the snowdrop is of the striving, hoping, longing Earth. Perhaps our highest poetry is the expression of our aspirations in the sympathetic forms of visible nature. Nor is this merely a longing for a restored Paradise; for even in the ordinary history of men, no man or woman that has fallen, can be restored to the position formerly held. Such must rise to a yet higher place, whence they can behold their former standing far beneath their feet. They must be restored by the attainment of something better than they ever possessed before, or not at all. If the law be a weariness, we must escape it by taking refuge with the spirit, for not otherwise can we fulfil the law than by being above the law. To escape the overhanging rocks of Sinai, we must climb to its secret top.

> " Is thy strait horizon dreary ?
>   Is thy foolish fancy chill ?
>   Change the feet that have grown weary,
>   For the wings that never will."

Thus, like one of the wandering knights searching the wide earth for the Sangreal, did he wander on, searching for his lost honour, or rather (for that he counted gone for ever) seeking unconsciously for the peace of mind which had departed from him, and taken with it, not the joy merely, but almost the possibility, of existence.

At last, when his little store was all but exhausted, he was employed by a market-gardener, in the neighbourhood of a large country town, to work in his garden, and sometimes take his vegetables to market. With him he continued for a few weeks, and wished for no change; until, one day, driving his cart through the town, he saw approaching him an elderly gentleman, whom he knew at once, by his gait and carriage, to be a military man. Now he had never seen his uncle the retired officer, but it struck him that this might be he; and under the tyranny of his passion for concealment, he fancied that, if it were he, he might recognise him by some family likeness— not considering the improbability of his looking at him. This fancy, with the painful effect which the sight of an officer, even in plain clothes, had upon him, recalling the torture of that frightful day, so overcame him, that he found himself at the other end of an alley before he recollected that he had the horse and cart in charge. This increased his difficulty; for now he dared not return, lest his inquiries after the vehicle, if the horse had strayed from the direct line, should attract attention, and cause interrogations which he would be unable to answer.   The fatal want of self-possession seemed again to ruin him.   He forsook the town by the nearest way, struck across the country to another line of road, and before he was missed, was miles away, still in a northerly direction.

But although he thus shunned the face of man, especially of any one who reminded him of the past, the loss of his reputation in their eyes was not the cause of his inward grief.   That would have been comparatively powerless to disturb him, had he not lost his own respect.   He quailed before his own thoughts; he was dis-honoured in his own eyes.   His perplexity had not yet sufficiently cleared away to allow him to see the extenuating circumstances of the case; not to say the fact, that the peculiar mental condition in which he was at the time, removed the case quite out of the class of ordinary instances of cowardice. He condemned himself more severely than any of his judges would have dared; remembering that portion of his mental sensations which had savoured of fear, and forgetting the causes which had produced it. He judged himself a man stained with the foulest blot that could cleave to a soldier's name, a blot which nothing but death, not even death, could efface. But, inwardly condemned and outwardly degraded, his dread of recognition was intense; and feeling that he was in more danger of being discovered where the population was sparser, he resolved to hide himself once more in the midst of poverty; and, with this view, found his way to one of the largest of the manufacturing towns.

He reached it during the strike of a great part of the workmen; so that, though he found some difficulty in procuring employment, as might be expected from his ignorance of machine-labour, he yet was sooner successful than he would otherwise have been. Possessed of a natural aptitude for mechanical operations, he soon became a tolerable workman; and he found that his previous education assisted to the fitting execution of those operations even which were most purely mechanical.

He found also, at first, that the unrelaxing attention requisite for the mastering of the many niceties of his work, of necessity drew his mind somewhat from its brooding over his misfortune, hitherto almost ceaseless. Every now and then, however, a pang would shoot suddenly to his heart, and turn his face pale, even before his consciousness had time to inquire what was the matter. So by degrees, as attention became less necessary, and the nervo-mechanical action of his system increased with use, his thoughts again returned to their old misery. He would wake at

night in his poor room, with the feeling that a
ghostly nightmare sat on his soul; that a want—a
loss—miserable, fearful—was present; that something of his heart was gone from him; and through
the darkness he would hear the snap of the break-
ing sword, and lie for a moment overwhelmed
beneath the assurance of the incredible fact.
Could it be true that *he* was a coward? that *his*
honour was gone, and in its place a stain? that *he*
was a thing for men—and worse, for women—to
point the finger at, laughing bitter laughter?
Never lover or husband could have mourned with
the same desolation over the departure of the
loved; the girl alone, weeping scorching tears
over *her* degradation, could resemble him in his
agony, as he lay on his bed, and wept and
moaned.

His sufferings had returned with the greater
weight, that he was no longer upheld by the

"divine air" and the open heavens, whose sunlight now only reached him late in an afternoon, as he stood at his loom, through windows so coated with dust that they looked like frosted glass; showing, as it passed through the air to fall on the dirty floor, how the breath of life was thick with dust of iron and wood, and films of cotton; amidst which his senses were now too much dulled by custom to detect the exhalations from greasy wheels and overtasked human-kind. Nor could he find comfort in the society of his fellow-labourers. True, it was a kind of comfort to have those near him who could not know of his grief; but there was so little in common between them, that any interchange of thought was impossible. At least, so it seemed to him. Yet sometimes his longing for human companionship would drive him out of his dreary room at night, and send him wandering through the lower part of the town, where he would gaze wistfully on the miserable faces that passed him, as if looking for some one—some angel, even there—to speak good will to his hungry heart.

Once he entered one of those gin-palaces, which, like the golden gates of hell, entice the miserable to worse misery, and seated himself close to a half tipsy, good-natured wretch, who made room for him on a bench by the wall. He was comforted even by this proximity to one who would not repel him. But soon the paintings of warlike action—of knights, and horses, and mighty deeds done with battle-axe and broad-sword, which adorned the panels all round, drove him forth even from this heaven of the damned ; yet not before the impious thought had arisen in his heart, that the brilliantly painted and sculptured roof, with the gilded vine-leaves and bunches of grapes trained up the windows, all lighted with the

great shining chandeliers, was only a microcosmic
repetition of the bright heavens and the glowing
earth, that overhung and surrounded the misery of
man. But the memory of how kindly they had
comforted and elevated him, at one period of his
painful history, not only banished the wicked
thought, but brought him more quiet, in the resurrection of a past blessing, than he had known for
some time. The period, however, was now at
hand, when a new grief, followed by a new and
more elevated activity, was to do its part towards
the closing up of the fountain of bitterness.

Amongst his fellow-labourers, he had for a short
time taken some interest in observing a young
woman, who had lately joined them. There was
nothing remarkable about her, except what at first
sight seemed a remarkable plainness. A slight
scar over one of her rather prominent eyebrows,
increased this impression of plainness. But the

first day had not passed, before he began to see that there was something not altogether common in those deep eyes; and the plain look vanished before a closer observation, which also discovered, in the forehead and the lines of the mouth, traces of sorrow or other suffering. There was an expression, too, in the whole face, of fixedness of purpose, without any hardness of determination. Her countenance altogether seemed the index to an interesting mental history. Signs of mental trouble were always an attraction to him; in this case so great, that he overcame his shyness, and spoke to her one evening as they left the works. He often walked home with her after that; as, indeed, was natural, seeing that she occupied an attic in the same poor lodging-house in which he lived himself. The street did not bear the best character; nor, indeed, would the occupations of all the inmates of the house have stood investigation; but so retiring and quiet was this girl, and so seldom did she go abroad after work-hours, that he had not discovered till then, that she lived in the same street, not to say the same house, with himself.

He soon learned her history—a very common one as to outward events, but not surely insignificant because common. Her father and mother were both dead, and hence she had to find her livelihood alone, and amidst associations which were always disagreeable, and sometimes painful. Her quick womanly instinct must have discovered that he too had a history; for though, his mental prostration favouring the operation of outward influences, he had greatly approximated in appearance to those amongst whom he laboured, there were yet signs, besides the educated accent of his speech, which would have distinguished him to an observer; but she put no questions to him nor made any approach towards seeking a return of the confidence she reposed in him. It was a sensible alleviation to his sufferings to hear her kind voice, and look in her gentle face, as they walked.home together; and at length the expectation of this pleasure began to present itself, in the midst of the busy, dreary work-hours, as the shadow of a heaven to close up the dismal, uninteresting day.

But one morning he missed her from her place, and a keener pain passed through him than he had felt of late; for he knew that the Plague was abroad, feeding in the low stagnant places of human abode; and he had but too much reason to dread that she might be now struggling in its grasp. He seized the first opportunity of slipping out and hurrying home. He sprang up stairs to her room. He found the door locked, but heard a faint moaning within. To avoid disturbing her, while determined to gain an entrance, he went down for the key of his own door, with which he succeeded in unlocking hers, and so crossed her threshold for the first time. There she lay on her bed, tossing in pain, and beginning to be delirious. Careless of his own life, and feeling that he could not die better than in helping the only friend he had; certain, likewise, of the difficulty of finding a nurse for one in this disease and of her station in life; and sure, likewise, that there could be no question of propriety, either in the circumstances with which they were surrounded, nor in this case of terrible fever almost as hopeless for her as dangerous to him, he instantly began the duties of a nurse, and returned no more to his employment. He had a little money in his possession, for he could not, in the way in which he lived, spend all his wages; so he proceeded to make her as comfortable as he could, with all the pent-up tenderness of a loving heart finding an outle at length. When a boy at home, he had often taken the place of nurse, and he felt quite capable of performing its duties. Nor was his boyhood far behind yet, although the trials he had come through made it appear an age since he had lost his light heart. So he never left her bedside, except to procure what was necessary for her. She was too ill to oppose any of his measures, or to seek to prohibit his presence. Indeed, by the time he had returned with the first medicine, she was insensible; and she continued so through the whole of the following week, during which time he was constantly with her.

That action produces feeling is as often true as its converse; and it is not surprising that, while he smoothed the pillow for her head, he should have made a nest in his heart for the helpless girl. Slowly and unconsciously he learned to love her. The chasm between his early associations and the circumstances in which he found her, vanished as he drew near to the simple, essential womanhood. His heart saw hers and loved it; and he knew that, the centre once gained, he could, as from the fountain of life, as from the innermost secret of the holy place, the hidden germ of power and possibility, transform the outer intellect and outermost manners as he pleased. With what a thrill of joy, a feeling for a long time unknown to him, and till now never known in this form or with this intensity, the thought arose in his heart that here lay one who some day would love him; that he should have a place of refuge and rest; one to lie in his bosom and not despise him! " For," said he to himself, "I will call forth her soul from where it sleeps, like an unawakened echo, in an unknown cave;

and like a child; of whom I once dreamed, that was mine, and to my delight turned in fear from all besides, and clung to me, this soul of hers will run with bewildered, half-sleeping eyes, and tottering steps, but with a cry of joy on its lips, to me as the life-giver. She will cling to me and worship me. Then will I tell her, for she must know all, that I am low and contemptible; that I am an outcast from the world; and that if she receive me, she will be to me as God. And I will fall down at her feet and pray her for comfort, for life, for restoration to myself; and she will throw herself beside me, and weep and love me, I know. And we will go through life together, working hard, but for each other; and when we die, she shall lead me into Paradise, as the prize her angel-hand found cast on a desert shore, from the storm of winds and waves which I was too weak to resist—and raised, and tended, and saved." Often did such thoughts as these pass through his mind while watching by her bed; alternated, checked, and sometimes destroyed, by the fears which attended her precarious condition, but returning with every apparent betterment or hopeful symptom.

I will not stop to decide the nice question, how far the intention was right, of causing her to love him before she knew his story. If in the whole matter there was too much thought of self, my only apology is the sequel. One day, the ninth from the commencement of her illness, a letter arrived, addressed to her; which he, thinking he might prevent some inconvenience thereby, opened and read, in the confidence of that love which already made her and all belonging to her appear his own. It was from a soldier —*her lover*. It was plain that they had been betrothed before he left for the continent a year ago; but this was the first letter which he had written to her. It breathed changeless love, and hope, and confidence in her. He was so fascinated that he read it through without pause.

Laying it down, he sat pale, motionless, almost inanimate. From the hard-won, sunny heights, he was once more cast down into the shadow of death. The second storm of his life began, howling and raging, with yet more awful lulls between. "Is she not *mine?*" he said, in agony. "Do I not feel that she is mine? Who will watch over her as I? Who will kiss her soul to life as I? Shall she be torn away from me, when my soul seems to have dwelt with hers for ever in an eternal house? But have I not a right to her? Have I not given my life for hers? Is he not a soldier, and are there not many chances that he may never return? And it may be, that although they were engaged in word, soul has never touched soul with them; their love has never reached that point where it passes from the mortal to the immortal, the indissoluble: and so, in a sense, she may be yet free. Will he do for her what I will do? Shall this precious heart of hers, in which I see the buds of so many beauties, be left to wither and die?"

But here the voice within him cried out, "Art thou the disposer of destinies? Wilt thou, in a universe where the visible God hath died for the Truth's sake, do evil that a good, which he might neglect or overlook, may be gained? Leave thou her to Him, and do thou right." And he said within himself, "Now is the real trial for my life! Shall I conquer or no?" And his heart awoke and cried, "I will. God forgive me for wronging the poor soldier! A brave man, brave at least, is better for her than I."

A great strength arose within him, and lifted

him up to depart. "Surely I may kiss her once," he said. For the crisis was over and she slept. He stooped towards her face, but before he had reached her lips he saw her eyelids tremble; and he who had longed for the opening of those eyes, as of the gates of heaven, that she might love him, stricken now with fear lest she should love him, fled from her, before the eyelids that hid such strife and such victory from the unconscious maiden, had time to unclose. But it was agony—quietly to pack up his bundle of linen in the room below, when he knew she was lying awake above, with her dear, pale face, and living eyes! What remained of his money, except a few shillings, he put up in a scrap of paper, and went out with his bundle in his hand, first to seek a nurse for his friend, and then to go he knew not whither. He met the factory people with whom he had worked, going to dinner, and amongst them a girl who had herself but lately recovered from the fever, and was yet hardly able for work. She was the only friend the sick girl had seemed to have amongst the women at the factory, and she was easily persuaded to go and take charge of her. He put the money in her hand, begging her to use it for the invalid, and promising to send the equivalent of her wages for the time he thought she would have to wait on her. This he easily did by the sale of a ring, which, besides his mother's watch, was the only article of value he had retained. He begged her likewise not to mention his name in the matter; and was foolish enough to expect that she would entirely keep the promise she made him.

Wandering along the street, purposeless now and bereft, he spied a recruiting party at the door of a public-house; and on coming nearer, found, by one of those strange coincidences which do

occur in life, and which have possibly their root
in a hidden and wondrous law, that it was a
party, perhaps a remnant, of the very regiment
in which he had himself served, and in which his
misfortune had befallen him.   Almost simultaneously with the shock which the sight of the
well-known number on the soldiers' knapsacks
gave him, arose in his mind the romantic, ideal
thought, of enlisting in the ranks of this same
regiment, and recovering, as private soldier and
unknown, that honour which as officer he had lost.
To this determination, the new necessity in which
he now stood for action and change of life,
doubtless contributed, though unconsciously.   He
offered himself to the sergeant; and, notwithstanding that his dress indicated a mode of life
unsuitable as the antecedent to a soldier's, his
appearance, and the necessity for recruits com
bined, led to his easy acceptance.

The English armies were employed in expelling the enemy from an invaded and helpless country. Whatever might be the political motives which had induced the government to this measure, the young man was now able to feel that he could go and fight, individually and for his part, in the cause of liberty. He was free to possess his own motives for joining in the execution of the schemes of those who commanded his commanders.

With a heavy heart, but with more of inward hope and strength than he had ever known before, he marched with his comrades to the sea-port and embarked. It seemed to him that because he had done right in his last trial, here was a new glorious chance held out to his hand. True, it was a terrible change, to pass from a woman in whom he had hoped to find healing, into the society of rough men, to march with them, " *mit gleichem Tritt und Schritt,"* up to the bristling bayonets or the horrid vacancy of the cannon-mouth. But it was the only cure for the evil that consumed his life.

He reached the army in safety, and gave himself, with religious assiduity, to the smallest duties of his new position. No one had a brighter polish on his arms, or whiter belts than he. In the necessary movements, he soon became precise to a degree that attracted the attention of his officers; while his character was remarkable for all the virtues belonging to a perfect soldier.

One day, as he stood sentry, he saw the eyes of his colonel intently fixed on him. He felt his lip quiver, but he compressed and stilled it, and tried to look as unconscious as he could; which effort was assisted by the formal bearing required by his position. Now the colonel, such had been the losses of the regiment, had been promoted from a lieutenancy in the same, and had belonged to it at the time of the ensign's degradation. Indeed, had not the changes in the regiment been so great, he could hardly have escaped so long without discovery. But the poor fellow would have felt that his name was already free of reproach, if he had seen what followed on the close inspection which had awakened his apprehensions, and which, in fact, had convinced the colonel of his identity with the disgraced ensign. With a hasty and less soldierly step than usual, the colonel entered his tent, threw himself on his bed and wept like a child. When he rose he was overheard to say these words—and these only escaped his lips: "He is nobler than I."

But this officer showed himself worthy of commanding such men as this private; for right nobly did he understand and meet his feelings. He uttered no word of the discovery he had made, till years afterwards; but it soon began to be re-marked that whenever anything arduous, or in any manner distinguished, had to be done, this man was sure to be of the party appointed. In short, as often as he could, the colonel "set him in the fore-front of the battle." Passing through all with wonderful escape, he was soon as much noticed for his reckless bravery, as hitherto for his precision in the discharge of duties bringing only commendation and not honour. But his final lustration was at hand.

A great part of the army was hastening, by forced marches, to raise the siege of a town, which was already on the point of falling into the hands of the enemy. Forming one of a reconnoitring party, which preceded the main body at some considerable distance, he and his companions came suddenly upon one of the enemy's outposts,

occupying a high, and on one side precipitous
rock, a short way from the town, which it com-
manded. Retreat was impossible, for they were
already discovered, and the bullets were falling
amongst them like the first of a hail-storm. The
only possibility of escape remaining for them, was
a nearly hopeless improbability. It lay in forcing
the post on this steep rock ; which if they could
do before assistance came to the enemy, they
might, perhaps, be able to hold out, by means of
its defences, till the arrival of the army. Their
position was at once understood by all; and,
by a sudden, simultaneous impulse, they found
themselves half-way up the steep ascent, and in
the struggle of a close conflict, without being
aware of any order to that effect from their
officer. But their courage was of no avail; the
advantages of the place were too great; and in a
few minutes the whole party was cut to pieces,

or stretched helpless on the rock. Our youth had fallen amongst the foremost; for a musket ball had grazed his skull, and laid him insensible.

But consciousness slowly returned; and he succeeded at last in raising himself and looking around him. The place was deserted. A few of his friends, alive, but grievously wounded, lay near him. The rest were dead. It appeared that, learning the proximity of the English forces from this rencontre with part of their advanced guard, and dreading lest the town, which was on the point of surrendering, should after all be snatched from their grasp, the commander of the enemy's forces had ordered an immediate and general assault; and had for this purpose recalled from their outposts the whole of his troops thus stationed, that he might make the attempt with the utmost strength he could accumulate.

As the youth's power of vision returned, he

perceived from the height where he lay, that the town was already in the hands of the enemy. But looking down into the level space immediately below him, he started to his feet at once; for a girl, bare-headed, was fleeing towards the rock, pursued by several soldiers. "Aha!" said he, divining her purpose—the soldiers behind and the rock before her—"I will help you to die!" And he stooped and wrenched from the dead fingers of a sergeant, the sword which they clenched by the bloody hilt. A new throb of life pulsed through him to his very finger-tips; and on the brink of the unseen world he stood, with the blood rushing through his veins in a wild dance of excitement. One who lay near him wounded, but recovered afterwards, said that he looked like one inspired. With a keen eye he watched the chase. The girl drew nigh; and rushed up the path near which he was standing.

Close on her footsteps came the soldiers, the distance gradually lessening between them.

Not many paces higher up, was a narrower part of the ascent, where the path was confined by great stones, or pieces of rock. Here had been the chief defence in the preceding assault, and in it lay many bodies of his friends. Thither he went and took his stand.

On the girl came, over the dead, with rigid hands and flying feet, the bloodless skin drawn tight on her features, and her eyes awfully large and wild. She did not see him though she bounded past so near, that her hair flew in his eyes. "Never mind!" said he, "we shall meet soon." And he stepped into the narrow path just in time to face her pursuers—between her and them. Like the red lightning the bloody sword fell, and a man beneath it. Cling! clang! went the echoes in the rocks—and another man was down; for, in his excitement, he was a destroying angel to the breathless pursuers. His stature rose, his chest dilated; and as the third foe fell dead, the girl was safe; for her body lay a broken, empty, but undesecrated temple, at the foot of the rock. That moment his sword flew in shivers from his grasp. The next instant he fell, pierced to the heart; and his spirit rose triumphant, free, strong, and calm, above the stormy world, which at length lay vanquished beneath him.

THE GRAY WOLF.

THE GRAY WOLF.

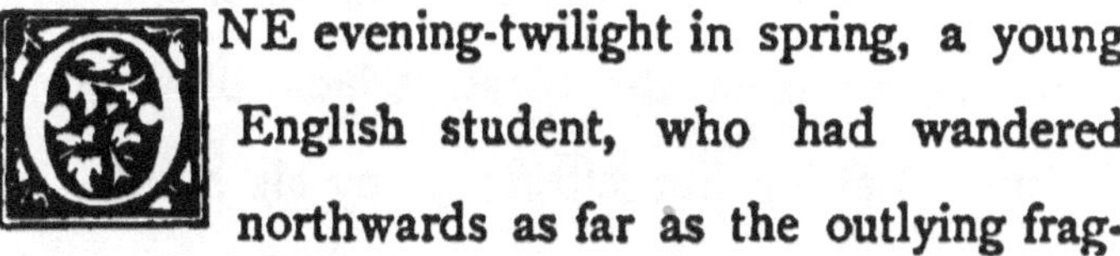NE evening-twilight in spring, a young English student, who had wandered northwards as far as the outlying fragments of Scotland called the Orkney and Shetland islands, found himself on a small island of the latter group, caught in a storm of wind and hail, which had come on suddenly. It was in vain to look about for any shelter; for not only did the storm entirely obscure the landscape, but there was nothing around him save a desert moss.

At length, however, as he walked on for mere walking's sake, he found himself on the verge of a cliff, and saw, over the brow of it, a few feet below him, a ledge of rock, where he might find some shelter from the blast, which blew from behind. Letting himself down by his hands, he alighted upon something that crunched beneath his tread, and found the bones of many small animals scattered about in front of a little cave in the rock, offering the refuge he sought. He went in, and sat upon a stone. The storm increased in violence, and as the darkness grew he became uneasy, for he did not relish the thought of spending the night in the cave. He had parted from his companions on the opposite side of the island, and it added to his uneasiness that they must be full of apprehension about him. At last there came a lull in the storm, and the same instant he heard a footfall, stealthy and light as that of a wild beast, upon the bones at the mouth of the cave. He started up in some fear, though the least thought might have satisfied him that there could be no very dangerous animals upon the island. Before he had time to think, however, the face of a woman appeared in the opening. Eagerly the wanderer spoke. She started at the sound of his voice. He could not see her well, because she was turned towards the darkness of the cave.

"Will you tell me how to find my way across the moor to Shielness?" he asked.

"You cannot find it to-night," she answered, in a sweet tone, and with a smile that bewitched him, revealing the whitest of teeth.

"What am I to do, then?" he asked.

"My mother will give you shelter, but that is all she has to offer."

"And that is far more than I expected a minute ago," he replied. "I shall be most grateful."

She turned in silence and left the cave. The youth followed.

She was barefooted, and her pretty brown feet went catlike over the sharp stones, as she led the way down a rocky path to the shore. Her garments were scanty and torn, and her hair blew tangled in the wind. She seemed about five and twenty, lithe and small. Her long fingers kept clutching and pulling nervously at her skirts as she went. Her face was very gray in complexion, and very worn, but delicately formed, and smooth-skinned. Her thin nostrils were tremulous as eyelids, and her lips, whose curves were faultless, had no colour to give sign of indwelling blood. What her eyes were like he could not see, for she had never lifted the delicate films of her eyelids.

At the foot of the cliff they came upon a little hut leaning against it, and having for its inner apartment a natural hollow within it. Smoke was spreading over the face of the rock, and the grateful odour of food gave hope to the hungry student. His guide opened the door of the cottage; he followed her in, and saw a woman bending over a fire in the middle of the floor. On the fire lay a large fish broiling. The daughter spoke a few words, and the mother turned and welcomed the stranger. She had an old and very wrinkled, but honest face, and looked troubled. She dusted the only chair in the cottage, and placed it for him by the side of the fire, opposite the one window, whence he saw a little patch of yellow sand over which the spent waves spread themselves out listlessly. Under this window there was a bench, upon which the daughter threw herself in an unusual posture, resting her chin upon her hand. A moment after the youth caught the first glimpse of her blue eyes. They were fixed upon him with a strange look of greed, amounting to craving, but as if aware that they belied or betrayed her, she dropped them instantly. The moment she veiled them, her face, notwithstanding its colourless complexion, was almost beautiful.

When the fish was ready, the old woman wiped the deal table, steadied it upon the uneven floor, and covered it with a piece of fine table-linen. She then laid the fish on a wooden platter, and invited the guest to help himself. Seeing no other provision, he pulled from his pocket a hunting knife, and divided a portion from the fish, offering it to the mother first.

"Come, my lamb," said the old woman; and the daughter approached the table. But her nostrils and mouth quivered with disgust.

The next moment she turned and hurried from the hut.

"She doesn't like fish," said the old woman, "and I haven't anything else to give her."

"She does not seem in good health," he rejoined.

The woman answered only with a sigh, and they ate their fish with the help of a little rye-bread. As they finished their supper, the youth heard the sound as of the pattering of a dog's feet upon the sand close to the door; but ere he had time to look out of the window, the door opened and the young woman entered. She looked better, perhaps from having just washed her face. She drew a stool to the corner of the fire opposite him. But as she sat down, to his bewilderment, and even horror, the student spied a single drop of blood on her white skin within her torn dress. The woman brought out a jar of whisky, put a rusty old kettle on the fire, and took her place in front of it. As soon as the water boiled, she proceeded to make some toddy in a wooden bowl.

Meantime the youth could not take his eyes off the young woman, so that at length he found himself fascinated, or rather bewitched. She kept her eyes for the most part veiled with the loveliest eyelids fringed with darkest lashes, and he gazed entranced ; for the red glow of the little oil-lamp covered all the strangeness of her complexion. But as soon as he met a stolen glance out of those eyes unveiled, his soul shuddered within him. Lovely face and craving eyes alternated fascination and repulsion.

The mother placed the bowl in his hands. He drank sparingly, and passed it to the girl. She lifted it to her lips, and as she tasted—only tasted it—looked at him. He thought the drink must have been drugged and have affected his brain. Her hair smoothed itself back, and drew her forehead backwards with it ; while the lower part of her face projected towards the bowl, revealing, ere she sipped, her dazzling teeth in strange prominence.   But the same moment the vision vanished; she returned the vessel to her mother, and rising, hurried out of the cottage.

Then the old woman pointed to a bed of heather in one corner with a murmured apology; and the student, wearied both with the fatigues of the day and the strangeness of the night, threw himself upon it, wrapped in his cloak. The moment he lay down, the storm began afresh, and the wind blew so keenly through the crannies of the hut, that it was only by drawing his cloak over his head that he could protect himself from its currents. Unable to sleep, he lay listening to the uproar which grew in violence, till the spray was dashing against the window. At length the door opened, and the young woman came in, made up the fire, drew the bench before it, and lay down in the same strange posture, with her chin propped on her hand and elbow, and her face turned towards the youth. He moved a little; she dropped her head, and lay on her face, with her arms crossed beneath her forehead. The mother had disappeared.

Drowsiness crept over him. A movement of the bench roused him, and he fancied he saw some four-footed creature as tall as a large dog trot quietly out of the door. He was sure he felt a rush of cold wind. Gazing fixedly through the darkness, he thought he saw the eyes of the damsel encountering his, but a glow from the falling together of the remnants of the fire, revealed clearly enough that the bench was vacant. Wondering what could have made her go out in such a storm, he fell fast asleep.

In the middle of the night he felt a pain in his shoulder, came broad awake, and saw the gleaming eyes and grinning teeth of some animal close to his face. Its claws were in his shoulder, and its mouth in the act of seeking his throat. Before it had fixed its fangs, however, he had its throat in one hand, and sought his knife with the other. A terrible struggle followed ; but regardless of the tearing claws, he found and opened his knife. He had made one futile stab, and was drawing it for a surer, when, with a spring of the whole body, and one wildly-contorted effort, the creature twisted its neck from his hold, and with something betwixt a scream and a howl, darted from him. Again he heard the door open ; again the wind blew in upon him, and it continued blowing ; a sheet of spray dashed across the floor, and over his face. He sprung from his couch and bounded to the door.

It was a wild night—dark, but for the flash of whiteness from the waves as they broke within a few yards of the cottage ; the wind was raving, and the rain pouring down the air. A gruesome sound as of mingled weeping and howling came from somewhere in the dark. He turned again into the hut and closed the door, but could find no way of securing it.

The lamp was nearly out, and he could not be certain whether the form of the young woman was upon the bench or not. Overcoming a strong repugnance, he approached it, and put out his hands—there was nothing there. He sat down and waited for the daylight: he dared not sleep any more.

When the day dawned at length, he went out yet again, and looked around. The morning was dim and gusty and gray. The wind had fallen, but the waves were tossing wildly. He wandered up and down the little strand, longing for more light.

At length he heard a movement in the cottage. By and by the voice of the old woman called to him from the door.

"You're up early, sir. I doubt you didn't sleep well."

"Not very well," he answered. "But where is your daughter?"

"She's not awake yet," said the mother. "I'm afraid I have but a poor breakfast for you. But you'll take a dram and a bit of fish. It's all I've got."

Unwilling to hurt her, though hardly in good appetite, he sat down at the table. While they were eating, the daughter came in, but turned her face away and went to the further end of the hut. When she came forward after a minute or two, the youth saw that her hair was drenched, and her face whiter than before. She looked ill and faint, and when she raised her eyes, all their fierceness had vanished, and sadness had taken its place. Her neck was now covered with a cotton handkerchief. She was modestly attentive to him, and no longer shunned his gaze. He was gradually yielding to the temptation of braving another night in the hut, and seeing what would follow, when the old woman spoke.

"The weather will be broken all day, sir," she said. "You had better be going, or your friends will leave without you."

Ere he could answer, he saw such a beseeching glance on the face of the girl, that he hesitated, confused. Glancing at the mother, he saw the flash of wrath in her face. She rose and approached her daughter, with her hand lifted to strike her. The young woman stooped her head with a cry. He darted round the table to interpose between them. But the mother had caught hold of her; the handkerchief had fallen from her neck; and the youth saw five blue bruises on her lovely throat—the marks of the four fingers and the thumb of a left hand. With a cry of horror he darted from the house, but as he reached the door he turned. His hostess was lying motionless on the floor, and a huge gray wolf came bounding after him.

There was no weapon at hand; and if there had been, his inborn chivalry would never have allowed him to harm a woman even under the guise of a wolf. Instinctively, he set himself firm, leaning a little forward, with half outstretched arms, and hands curved ready to clutch again at the throat upon which he had left those pitiful marks. But the creature as she sprung eluded his grasp, and just as he expected to feel her fangs, he found a woman weeping on his bosom, with her arms around his neck. The next instant, the gray wolf broke from him, and bounded howling up the cliff. Recovering himself as he best might, the youth followed, for it was the only way to the moor above, across which he must now make his way to find his companions.

All at once he heard the sound of a crunching of bones—not as if a creature was eating them, but as if they were ground by the teeth of rage and disappointment: looking up, he saw close above him the mouth of the little cavern in which he had taken refuge the day before. Summoning all his resolution, he passed it slowly and softly. From within came the sounds of a mingled moaning and growling.

Having reached the top, he ran at full speed for some distance across the moor before venturing to look behind him. When at length he did so, he saw, against the sky, the girl standing on the edge of the cliff, wringing her hands. One solitary wail crossed the space between. She made no attempt to follow him, and he reached the opposite shore in safety.

UNCLE CORNELIUS HIS
STORY.

UNCLE CORNELIUS HIS STORY.

T was a dull evening in November. A drizzling mist had been falling all day about the old farm. Harry Heywood and his two sisters sat in the house-place, expecting a visit from their uncle, Cornelius Heywood. This uncle lived alone, occupying the first floor above a chemist's shop in the town, and had just enough of money over to buy books that nobody seemed ever to have heard of but himself; for he was a student in all those regions of speculation in which anything to be called knowledge is impossible.

"What a dreary night!" said Kate. "I wish uncle would come and tell us a story."

"A cheerful wish," said Harry. "Uncle Cornie is a lively companion,—isn't he? He can't even blunder through a Joe Miller without tacking a moral to it, and then trying to persuade you that the joke of it depends on the moral."

"Here he comes!" said Kate, as three distinct blows with the knob of his walking-stick announced the arrival of Uncle Cornelius. She ran to the door to open it.

The air had been very still all day, but as he entered he seemed to have brought the wind with him, for the first moan of it pressed against rather than shook the casement of the low-ceiled room.

Uncle Cornelius was very tall, and very thin, and very pale, with large gray eyes that looked greatly larger because he wore spectacles of the most delicate hair-steel, with the largest pebble-eyes that ever were seen. He gave them a kindly greeting, but too much in earnest even in shaking hands to smile over it. He sat down in the arm-chair by the chimney corner.

I have been particular in my description of him, in order that my reader may give due weight to his words. I am such a believer in words, that I believe everything depends on who says them. Uncle Cornelius Heywood's story told word for word by Uncle Timothy Warren, would not have been the same story at all. Not one of the listeners would have believed a syllable of it from the lips of round-bodied, red-faced, small-eyed, little Uncle Tim; whereas from Uncle Cornie,— disbelieve one of his stories if you could!

One word more concerning him. His interest in everything conjectured or believed relative to the awful borderland of this world and the next, was only equalled by his disgust at the vulgar, unimaginative forms which curiosity about such subjects has assumed in the present day. With a yearning after the unseen like that of a child for the lifting of the curtain of a theatre, he declared that, rather than accept such a spirit-world as the would-be seers of the nineteenth century thought or pretended to reveal,—the prophets of a pauperized, workhouse immortality, invented by a poverty-stricken soul, and a sense so greedy that it would gorge on carrion,—he would rejoice to believe that a man had just as much of a soul as the cabbage of Iamblichus, namely, an aerial double of his body.

"I'm so glad you're come, uncle!" said Kate. "Why wouldn't you come to dinner? We have been so gloomy!"

"Well, Katey, you know I don't admire eating. I never could bear to see a cow tearing up the grass with her long tongue." As he spoke he looked very much like a cow. He had a way of opening his jaws while he kept his lips closely pressed together, that made his cheeks fall in, and his face look awfully long and dismal. "I consider eating," he went on, "such an animal exercise that it ought always to be performed in private. You never saw me dine, Kate."

"Never, uncle; but I have seen you drink;—nothing but water, I must confess."

"Yes, that is another affair. According to one eye-witness, that is no more than the disembodied can do. I must confess, however, that, although well attested, the story is to me scarcely credible. Fancy a glass of Bavarian beer lifted into the air without a visible hand, turned upside down, and set empty on the table!—and no splash on the floor or anywhere else!"

A solitary gleam of humour shone through the great eyes of the spectacles as he spoke.

"Oh, uncle! how can you believe such nonsense!" said Janet.

"I did not say I believed it,—did I? But why not? The story has at least a touch of imagination in it."

"That is a strange reason for believing a thing, uncle," said Harry.

"You might have a worse, Harry. I grant it is not sufficient; but it is better than that common-place aspect which is the ground of most faith. I believe I did say that the story puzzled me."

"But how can you give it any quarter at all, uncle?"

"It does me no harm. There it is,—between the boards of an old German book. There let it remain."

"Well, you will never persuade me to believe such things," said Janet.

"Wait till I ask you, Janet," returned her uncle, gravely. "I have not the slightest desire to convince you. How did we get into this unprofitable current of talk ? We will change it at once. How are consols, Harry ?"

"Oh, uncle!" said Kate, "we were longing for a story, and just as I thought you were coming to one, off you go to consols!"

"I thought a ghost story at least was coming," said Janet.

"You did your best to stop it, Janet," said Harry.

Janet began an angry retort, but Cornelius interrupted her. "You never heard me tell a ghost story, Janet."

"You have just told one about a drinking ghost, uncle," said Janet,—in such a tone that Cornelius replied :

"Well, take that for your story, and let us talk of something else."

Janet apparently saw that she had been rude, and said as sweetly as she might,—"Ah ! but you didn't make that one, uncle.   You got it out of a German book."

"Make it!—Make a ghost story!" repeated Cornelius.   "No; that I never did."

"Such things are not to be trifled with, are they?" said Janet.

"I at least have no inclination to trifle with them."

"But, really and truly, uncle," persisted Janet, "you don't believe in such things?"

"Why should I either believe or disbelieve in them? They are not essential to salvation, I presume."

"You must do the one or the other, I suppose."

"I beg your pardon. You suppose wrong. It would take twice the proof I have ever had to make me believe in them ; and exactly your prejudice, and allow me to say ignorance, to make me disbelieve in them.   Neither is within my reach.

I postpone judgment. But you, young people, of course, are wiser, and know all about the question."

"Oh, uncle! I'm so sorry!" said Kate. "I am sure I did not mean to vex you."

"Not at all, not at all, my dear.—It wasn't you."

"Do you know," Kate went on, anxious to prevent anything unpleasant, for there was something very black perched on Janet's forehead,—"I have taken to reading about that kind of thing."

"I beg you will give it up at once. You will bewilder your brains till you are ready to believe anything, if only it be absurd enough. Nay, you may come to find the element of vulgarity essential to belief. I should be sorry to the heart to believe concerning a horse or dog what they tell you now-a-days about Shakspeare and Burns. What have you been reading, my girl?"

"Don't be alarmed, uncle. Only some Highland legends, which are too absurd either for my belief or for your theories."

"I don't know that, Kate."

"Why, what could you do with such shapeless creatures as haunt their fords and pools for instance? They are as featureless as the faces of the mountains."

"And so much the more terrible."

"But that does not make it easier to believe in them," said Harry.

"I only said," returned his uncle, "that their shapelessness adds to their horror."

"But you allowed,—almost, at least, uncle," said Kate, "that you could find a place in your theories even for those shapeless creatures."

Cornelius sat silent for a moment; then, having first doubled the length of his face, and restored it to its natural condition, said thoughtfully,—

"I suspect, Katey, if you were to come upon

an ichthyosaurus or a pterodactyl asleep in the shrubbery, you would hardly expect your report of it to be believed all at once either by Harry or Janet."

"I suppose not, uncle. But I can't see what——"

"Of course such a thing could not happen here and now. But there was a time when and a place where such a thing may have happened. Indeed, in my time, a traveller or two have got pretty soundly disbelieved for reporting what they saw,—the last of an expiring race, which had strayed over the natural verge of its history, coming to life in some neglected swamp, itself a remnant of the slime of Chaos."

"I never heard you talk like that before, uncle," said Harry. "If you go on like that, you'll land me in a swamp, I'm afraid."

"I wasn't talking to you at all, Harry. Kate

challenged me to find a place for kelpies, and such like, in the theories she does me the honour of supposing I cultivate."

"Then you think, uncle, that all these stories are only legends which, if you could follow them up, would lead you back to some one of the awful monsters that have since quite disappeared from the earth."

"It is possible those stories may be such legends; but that was not what I intended to lead you to. I gave you that only as something like what I am going to say now. What if,— mind, I only suggest it,—what if the direful creatures, whose report lingers in these tales, should have an origin far older still? What if they were the remnants of a vanishing period of the earth's history long antecedent to the birth of mastodon and iguanodon; a stage, namely, when the world, as we call it, had not yet become quite visible, was not yet so far finished as to part from the invisible world that was its mother, and which, on its part, had not then become quite invisible,—was only almost such ; and when, as a credible consequence, strange shapes of those now invisible regions, Gorgons and Chimæras dire, might be expected to gloom out occasionally from the awful Fauna of an ever-generating world upon that one which was being born of it. Hence, the life-periods of a world being long and slow, some of these huge, unformed bulks of half-created matter might, somehow, like the megatherium of later times,—a baby creation to them,—roll at age-long intervals, clothed in a mighty terror of shapeless-ness, into the half-recognition of human beings, whose consternation at the uncertain vision were barrier enough to prevent all further knowledge of its substance."

s

" I begin to have some notion of your meaning, uncle," said Kate.

" But then," said Janet, "all that must be over by this time.   That world has been invisible now for many years."

" Ever since you were born, I suppose, Janet. The changes of a world are not to be measured by the changes of its generations."

"Oh, but, uncle, there can't be any such things. You know that as well as I do."

" Yes, just as well, and no better."

"There can't be any ghosts now.   Nobody believes such things."

"Oh, as to ghosts, that is quite another thing. I did not know you were talking with reference to them.   It is no wonder if one can get nothing sensible out of you, Janet, when your discrimination is no greater than to lump everything marvellous, kelpies, ghosts, vampires, doubles, witches, fairies, nightmares, and I don't know what all, under the one head of ghosts; and we hadn't been saying a word about them. If one were to disprove to you the existence of the afreets of Eastern tales, you would consider the whole argument concerning the reappearance of the departed upset. I congratulate you on your powers of analysis and induction, Miss Janet. But it matters very little whether we believe in ghosts, as you say, or not, provided we believe that we are ghosts,—that within this body, which so many people are ready to consider their own very selves, there lies a ghostly embryo, at least, which has an inner side to it God only can see, which says I concerning itself, and which will soon have to know whether or not it can appear to those whom it has left behind, and thus solve the question of ghosts for itself, at least."

"Then you do believe in ghosts, uncle?"

said Janet, in a tone that certainly was not respectful.

"Surely I said nothing of the sort, Janet. The man most convinced that he had himself had such an interview as you hint at, would find,— ought to find it impossible to convince any one else of it."

"You are quite out of my depth, uncle," said Harry. "Surely any honest man ought to be believed?"

"Honesty is not all, by any means, that is necessary to being believed. It is impossible to convey a conviction of anything. All you can do is to convey a conviction that you are convinced. Of course, what satisfied you might satisfy another; but, till you can present him with the sources of your conviction, you cannot present him with the conviction,—and perhaps not even then."

"You can tell him all about it, can't you?"

" Is telling a man about a ghost, affording him the source of your conviction ? Is it the same as a ghost appearing to him ? Really, Harry !—You cannot even convey the impression a dream has made upon you."

" But isn't that just because it is only a dream ? "

" Not at all. The impression may be deeper and clearer on your mind than any fact of the next morning will make. You will forget the next day altogether, but the impression of the dream will remain through all the following whirl and storm of what you call facts. Now a conviction may be likened to a deep impression on the judgment or the reason, or both. No one can feel it but the person who is convinced. It cannot be conveyed."

" I fancy that is just what those who believe in spirit-rapping would say."

"There are the true and false of convictions, as of everything else. I mean that a man may take that for a conviction in his own mind which is not a conviction, but only resembles one. But those to whom you refer profess to appeal to facts. It is on the ground of those facts, and with the more earnestness the more reason they can give for receiving them as facts, that I refuse all their deductions with abhorrence. I mean that, if what they say is true, the thinker must reject with contempt the claim to anything like revelation therein."

"Then you do not believe in ghosts, after all?" said Kate, in a tone of surprise.

"I did not say so, my dear. Will you be reasonable, or will you not?"

"Dear uncle, do tell us what you really think."

"I have been telling you what I think ever

since I came, Katey; and you won't take in a word I say."

" I have been taking in every word, uncle, and trying hard to understand it as well.—Did you ever see a ghost, uncle ?"

Cornelius Heywood was silent. He shut his lips and opened his jaws till his cheeks almost met in the vacuum. A strange expression crossed the strange countenance, and the great eyes of his spectacles looked as if, at the very moment, they were seeing something no other spectacles could see. Then his jaws closed with a snap, his countenance brightened, a flash of humour came through the goggle eyes of pebble, and, at length, he actually smiled as he said—" Really, Katey, you must take me for a simpleton !"

" How, uncle ?"

" To think, if I had ever seen a ghost, I would confess the fact before a set of creatures like you,

—all spinning your webs like so many spiders to catch and devour old Daddy Longlegs."

By this time Harry had grown quite grave. "Indeed, I am very sorry, uncle," he said, "if I have deserved such a rebuke."

"No, no, my boy," said Cornelius; "I did not mean it more than half. If I had meant it, I would not have said it. If you really would like ——" Here he paused.

"Indeed we should, uncle," said Kate, earnestly. "You should have heard what we were saying just before you came in."

"All you were saying, Katey?"

"Yes," answered Kate, thoughtfully. "The worst we said was that you could not tell a story without——well, we did say tacking a moral to it."

"Well, well! I mustn't push it. A man has no right to know what people say about him. It unfits him for occupying his real position amongst them. He, least of all, has anything to do with it. If his friends won't defend him, he can't defend himself. Besides, what people say is so often untrue!—I don't mean to others, but to themselves. Their hearts are more honest than their mouths. But Janet doesn't want a strange story, I am sure."

Janet certainly was not one to have chosen for a listener to such a tale. Her eyes were so small that no satisfaction could possibly come of it. "Oh! I don't mind, uncle," she said, with half-affected indifference, as she searched in her box for silk to mend her gloves.

"You are not very encouraging, I must say," returned her uncle, making another cow-face.

"I will go away, if you like," said Janet, pretending to rise.

"No, never mind," said her uncle hastily.

"If you don't want me to tell it, I want you to hear it; and, before I have done, that may have come to the same thing perhaps."

"Then you really are going to tell us a ghost-story!" said Kate, drawing her chair nearer to her uncle's; and then, finding this did not satisfy her sense of propinquity to the source of the expected pleasure, drawing a stool from the corner, and seating herself almost on the hearth-rug at his knee.

"I did not say so," returned Cornelius, once more. "I said I would tell you a strange story. You may call it a ghost-story if you like; I do not pretend to determine what it is. I confess it will look like one though."

After so many delays, Uncle Cornelius now plunged almost hurriedly into his narration.

"In the year 1820," he said, "in the month of August, I fell in love." Here the girls glanced at each other.   The idea of Uncle Cornie in love, and in the very same century in which they were now listening to the confession, was too astonishing to pass without ocular remark ; but, if he observed it, he took no notice of it ; he did not even pause.   "In the month of September, I was refused.   Consequently, in the month of October, I was ready to fall in love again.   Take particular care of yourself, Harry, for a whole month, at least, after your first disappointment ; for you will never be more likely to do a foolish thing. Please yourself after the second.   If you are silly then, you may take what you get, for you will deserve it,—except it be good fortune."

"Did you do a foolish thing then, uncle?" asked Harry, demurely.

"I did, as you will see ; for I fell in love again.'

" I don't see anything so very foolish in that."

"I have repented it since, though. Don't interrupt me again, please. In the middle of October, then, in the year 1820, in the evening, I was walking across Russell Square, on my way home from the British Museum, where I had been reading all day. You see I have a full intention of being precise, Janet."

"I'm sure I don't know why you make the remark to me, uncle," said Janet, with an involuntary toss of her head. Her uncle only went on with his narrative.

"I begin at the very beginning of my story," he said; "for I want to be particular as to everything that can appear to have had anything to do with what came afterwards. I had been reading, I say, all the morning in the British Museum; and, as I walked, I took off my spectacles to ease my eyes. I need not tell you that I am short-sighted now, for that you know well enough. But I must tell you that I was short-sighted then, and helpless enough without my spectacles, although I was not quite so much so as I am now;—for I find it all nonsense about short-sighted eyes improving with age. Well, I was walking along the south side of Russell Square, with my spectacles in my hand, and feeling a little bewildered in consequence,—for it was quite the dusk of the evening, and short-sighted people require more light than others. I was feeling, in fact, almost blind. I had got more than half-way to the other side, when, from the crossing that cuts off the corner in the direction of Montagu Place, just as I was about to turn towards it, an old lady stepped upon the kerbstone of the pavement, looked at me for a moment, and passed,—an occurrence not very remarkable, certainly. But the lady was remarkable, and so was her dress. I am not good at observing, and I am still worse at describing dress, therefore, I can only say that hers reminded me of an old picture,—that is, I had never seen anything like it, except in old pictures. She had no bonnet, and looked as if she had walked straight out of an ancient drawing-room in her evening attire. Of her face I shall say nothing now. The next instant I met a man on the crossing, who stopped and addressed me. So short-sighted was I that, although I recognized his voice as one I ought to know, I could not identify him until I had put on my spectacles, which I did instinctively in the act of returning his greeting. At the same moment I glanced over my shoulder after the old lady. She was nowhere to be seen.

"'What are you looking at?' asked James Iletheridge.

"'I was looking after that old lady,' I answered, 'but I can't see her.'

"'What old lady?' said Hetheridge, with just a touch of impatience.

"'You must have seen her,' I returned. 'You were not more than three yards behind her.'

"'Where is she then?'

"'She must have gone down one of the areas, I think. But she looked a lady, though an old-fashioned one.'

"'Have you been dining?' asked James in a tone of doubtful inquiry.

"'No,' I replied, not suspecting the in-sinuation; 'I have only just come from the Museum.'

"'Then I advise you to call on your medical man before you go home.'

"'Medical man!' I returned; 'I have no medical man. What do you mean? I never was better in my life.'

"'I mean that there was no old lady. It was

an illusion, and that indicates something wrong. Besides, you did not know me when I spoke to you.'

" ' That is nothing,' I returned. ' I had just taken off my spectacles, and without them I shouldn't know my own father.'

" ' How was it you saw the old lady, then ? '

" The affair was growing serious under my friend's cross-questioning. I did not at all like the idea of his supposing me subject to hallucinations. So I answered, with a laugh, ' Ah ! to be sure, that explains it. I am so blind without my spectacles, that I shouldn't know an old lady from a big dog.'

" ' There was no big dog,' said Hetheridge, shaking his head, as the fact for the first time dawned upon me that, although I had seen the old lady clearly enough to make a sketch of her, even to the features of her careworn, eager old face, I had not been able to recognise the well-known countenance of James Hetheridge.

" ' That's what comes of reading till the optic nerve is weakened,' he went on. ' You will cause yourself serious injury if you do not pull up in time. I'll tell you what ; I'm going home next week,—will you go with me ? '

" ' You are very kind,' I answered, not altogether rejecting the proposal, for I felt that a little change to the country would be pleasant, and I was quite my own master. For I had unfortunately means equal to my wants, and had no occasion to follow any profession,—not a very desirable thing for a young man, I can tell you, Master Harry. I need not keep you over the commonplaces of pressing and yielding. It is enough to say that he pressed and that I yielded. The day was fixed for our departure together ; but something or other, I forget what, occurred,

to make him advance the datë, and it was resolved that I should follow later in the month.

"It was a drizzly afternoon in the beginning of
the last week of October when I left the town of
Bradford in a postchaise to drive to Lewton
Grange, the property of my friend's father. I had
hardly left the town, and the twilight had only
begun to deepen, when, glancing from one of the
windows of the chaise, I fancied I saw, between
me and the hedge, the dim figure of a horse keeping pace with us. I thought, in the first interval
of unreason, that it was a shadow from my own
horse, but reminded myself the next moment that
there could be no shadow where there was no light.
When I looked again, I was at the first glance
convinced that my eyes had deceived me. At the
second, I believed once more that a shadowy something, with the movements of a horse in harness,
was keeping pace with us. I turned away again

with some discomfort, and not till we had reached an open moorland road, whence a little watery light was visible on the horizon, could I summon up courage enough to look out once more. Certainly then there was nothing to be seen, and I persuaded myself that it had been all a fancy, and lighted a cigar. With my feet on the cushions before me, I had soon lifted myself on the clouds of tobacco far above all the terrors of the night, and believed them banished for ever. But, my cigar coming to an end just as we turned into the avenue that led up to the Grange, I found myself once more glancing nervously out of the window. The moment the trees were about me, there was, if not a shadowy horse out there by the side of the chaise, yet certainly more than half that conviction in here in my consciousness. When I saw my friend, however, standing on the doorstep, dark against the glow of the hall-fire, I forgot all about it; and I need not add that I did not make it a subject of conversation when I entered, for I was well aware that it was essential to a man's reputation that his senses should be accurate, though his heart might without prejudice swarm with shadows, and his judgment be a very stable of hobbies.

"I was kindly received. Mrs. Hetheridge had been dead for some years, and Lætitia, the eldest of the family, was at the head of the household. She had two sisters, little more than girls. The father was a burly, yet gentlemanlike Yorkshire squire, who ate well, drank well, looked radiant, and hunted twice a week. In this pastime his son joined him when in the humour, which happened scarcely so often. I, who had never crossed a horse in my life, took his apology for not being able to mount me very coolly, assuring him that I would rather loiter about with a book than be in at the death of the best-hunted fox in . Yorkshire.

"I very soon found myself at home with the Hetheridges; and very soon again I began to find myself not so much at home; for Miss Hethe-ridge,—Lætitia as I soon ventured to call her,— was fascinating. I have told you, Katey, that there was a empty place in my heart. Look to the door then, Katey. That was what made me so ready to fall in love with Lætitia. Her figure was graceful, and I think, even now, her face would have been beautiful but for a certain contraction of the skin over the nostrils, suggest-ing an invisible thumb and forefinger pinching them, which repelled me, although I did not then know what it indicated. I had not been with her one evening before the impression it made on me had vanished, and that so entirely that I could hardly recall the perception of the peculiarity which had occasioned it. Her observation was remarkably keen, and her judgment generally correct. She had great confidence in it herself; nor was she devoid of sympathy with some of the forms of human imagination, only they never seemed to possess for her any relation to practical life. That was to be ordered by the judgment alone. I do not mean she ever said so. I am only giving the conclusions I came to afterwards. It is not necessary that .you should have any more thorough acquaintance with her mental character. One point in her moral nature, of especial consequence to my narrative, will show itself by and by.

"I did all I could to make myself agreeable to her, and the more I succeeded the more delightful she became in my eyes. We walked in the garden and grounds together; we read, or rather I read and she listened ;—read poetry,

Katey—sometimes till we could not read any more for certain hazinesses and huskinesses which look now, I am afraid, considerably more absurd than they really were, or even ought to look. In short, I considered myself thoroughly in love with her."

" And wasn't she in love with you, uncle ? "

" Don't interrupt me, child. I don't know. Honestly, I don't know. I hoped so then. I hope the contrary now. She liked me I am sure. That is not much to say. Liking is very pleasant and very cheap. Love is as rare as a star."

" I thought the stars were anything but rare, uncle."

" That's because you never went out to find one for yourself, Katey. They would prove a few miles apart then."

" But it would be big enough when I did find it."

" Right, my dear. That is the way with love.

—Lætitia was a good housekeeper. Everything was punctual as clockwork. I use the word advisedly. If her father, who was punctual to one date,—the dinner-hour,—made any remark to the contrary as he took up the carving-knife, Lætitia would instantly send one of her sisters to question the old clock in the hall, and report the time to half a minute. It was sure to be found that, if there was a mistake, the mistake was in the clock. But although it was certainly a virtue to have her household in such perfect order, it was not a virtue to be impatient with every infringement of its rules on the part of others. She was very severe, for instance, upon her two younger sisters if, the moment after the second bell had rung, they were not seated at the dinner-table, washed and aproned. Order was a very idol with her. Hence the house was too tidy for any sense of comfort. If you left an open book on the table, you would, on returning to the room a moment after, find it put aside. What the furniture of the drawing-room was like, I never saw; for not even on Christmas-Day, which was the last day I spent there, was it uncovered. Everything in it was kept in bibs and pinafores. Even the carpet was covered with a cold and slippery sheet of brown holland. Mr. Hetheridge never entered that room, and therein was wise. James remonstrated once. She answered him quite kindly, even playfully, but no change followed. What was worse, she made very wretched tea. Her father never took tea; neither did James. I was rather fond of it, but I soon gave it up. Everything her father partook of was first-rate. Everything else was somewhat poverty-stricken. My pleasure in Lætitia's society prevented me from making practical deductions from such trifles."

"I shouldn't have thought you knew anything about eating, uncle," said Janet.

"The less a man eats, the more he likes to have it good, Janet. In short,—there can be no harm in saying it now,—Lætitia was so far from being like the name of her baptism,—and most names are so good that they are worth thinking about; no children are named after bad ideas,—Lætitia was so far unlike hers as to be stingy,—an abominable fault. But, I repeat, the notion of such a fact was far from me then. And now for my story.

"The first of November was a very lovely day, quite one of the 'halcyon days' of 'St. Martin's summer.' I was sitting in a little arbour I had just discovered, with a book in my hand,—not reading, however, but day-dreaming,—when, lifting my eyes from the ground, I was startled to see, through a thin shrub in front of the arbour, what 'seemed the form of an old lady seated, apparently reading from a book on her knee. The sight instantly recalled the old lady of Russell Square. I started to my feet, and then, clear of the intervening bush, saw only a great stone such as abounded on the moors in the neighbourhood, with a lump of quartz set on the top of it. Some childish taste had put it there for an ornament. Smiling at my own folly, I sat down again, and reopened my book. After reading for a while, I glanced up again, and once more started to my feet, overcome by the fancy that there verily sat the old lady reading. You will say it indicated an excited condition of the brain. Possibly; but I was, as far as I can recall, quite collected and reasonable. I was almost vexed this second time, and sat down once more to my book. Still, every time I looked up, I was startled afresh. I doubt, however, if the trifle is worth mentioning, or has any significance even in relation to what followed.

"After dinner I strolled out by myself, leaving father and son over their claret. I did not drink wine; and from the lawn I could see the windows of the library, whither Lætitia commonly retired from the dinner-table. It was a very lovely soft night. There was no moon, but the stars looked wider awake than usual. Dew was falling, but the grass was not yet wet, and I wandered about on it for half an hour. The stillness was some-how strange. It had a wonderful feeling in it as if something were expected,—as if the quietness were the mould in which some event or other was about to be cast.

"Even then I was a reader of certain sorts of recondite lore. Suddenly I remembered that this was the eve of All Souls. This was the night on which the dead came out of their graves to visit their old homes. 'Poor dead!' I thought with myself; 'have you any place to call a home now? If you have, surely you will not wander back here, where all that you called home has either vanished or given itself to others, to be their home now and yours no more! What an awful doom the old fancy has allotted you! To dwell in your graves all the year, and creep out, this one night, to enter at the midnight door, left open for welcome! A poor welcome truly!—just an open door, a clean-swept floor, and a fire to warm your rain-sodden limbs! The household asleep, and the house-place swarming with the ghosts of ancient times,—the miser, the spendthrift, the profligate, the coquette,—for the good ghosts sleep, and are troubled with no waking like yours! Not one man, sleepless like yourselves, to question you, and be answered after the fashion of the old nursery rhyme;—

"' What makes your eyes so holed ?'
' I've lain so long among the mould.'
' What makes your feet so broad ?'
' I've walked more than ever I rode !'"

"'Yet who can tell?' I went on to myself. 'It may be your hell to return thus. It may be that only on this one night of all the year you can show yourselves to him who can see you, but that the place where you were wicked is the Hades to which you are doomed for ages.' I thought and thought till I began to feel the air alive about me, and was enveloped in the vapours that dim the eyes of those who strain them for one peep through the dull mica windows that will not open on the world of ghosts. At length I cast my fancies away, and fled from them to the library, where the bodily presence of Lætitia made the world of ghosts appear shadowy indeed.

"'What a reality there is about a bodily

presence!' I said to myself, as I took my chamber-candle in my hand. 'But what is there more real in a body?' I said again, as I crossed the hall. 'Surely nothing,' I went on, as I ascended the broad staircase to my room. 'The body must vanish. If there be a spirit, that will remain. A body can but vanish. A ghost can appear.'

"I woke in the morning with a sense of such discomfort as made me spring out of bed at once. My foot lighted upon my spectacles. How they came to be on the floor I could not tell, for I never took them off when I went to bed. When I lifted them I found they were in two pieces; the bridge was broken. This was awkward. I was so utterly helpless without them! Indeed, before I could lay my hand on my hair-brush I had to peer through one eye of the parted pair. When I looked at my watch after I was dressed,

I found I had risen an hour earlier than usual. I groped my way down stairs to spend the hour before breakfast in the library.

"No sooner was I seated with a book than I heard the voice of Lætitia scolding the butler, in no very gentle tones, for leaving the garden-door open all night. The moment I heard this, the strange occurrences I am about to relate began to dawn upon my memory. The door had been open the night long between All Saints and All Souls. In the middle of that night I awoke suddenly. I knew it was not the morning by the sensations I had, for the night feels altogether different from the morning. It was quite dark. My heart was beating violently, and I either hardly could or hardly dared breathe. A nameless terror was upon me, and my sense of hearing was, apparently by the force of its expectation, unnaturally roused and keen. There it was,—a slight noise in the room!—slight, but clear, and with an unknown significance about it! It was awful to think it would come again. I do believe it was only one of those creaks in the timbers which announce the torpid, age-long, sinking flow of every house back to the dust,—a motion to which the flow of the glacier is as a torrent, but which is no less inevitable and sure. Day and night it ceases not; but only in the night, when house and heart are still, do we hear it. No wonder it should sound fearful! for are we not the immortal dwellers in ever-crumbling clay? The clay is so near us, and yet not of us, that its every movement starts a fresh dismay. For what will its final ruin disclose? When it falls from about us, where shall we find that we have existed all the time?

"My skin tingled with the bursting of the moisture from its pores. Something was in the room beside me. A confused, indescribable sense of utter loneliness, and yet awful presence, was upon me, mingled with a dreary, hopeless desolation, as of burnt-out love and aimless life. All at once I found myself sitting up. The terror that a cold hand might be laid upon me, or a cold breath blow on me, or a corpse-like face bend down through the darkness over me, had broken my bonds!—I would meet half way whatever might be approaching. The moment that my will burst into action the terror began to ebb.

"The room in which I slept was a large one, perfectly dreary with tidiness. I did not know till afterwards that it was Lætitia's room, which she had given up to me rather than prepare another. The furniture, all but one article, was modern and commonplace. I could not help remarking to myself afterwards how utterly void the room was of the nameless charm of feminine occupancy. I had seen nothing to wake a suspicion of its being a lady's room. The article I have excepted was an ancient bureau, elaborate and ornate, which stood on one side of the large bow window. The very morning before, I had seen a bunch of keys hanging from the upper part of it, and had peeped in. Finding, however, that the pigeon-holes were full of papers, I closed it at once. I should have been glad to use it, but clearly it was not for me. At that bureau the figure of a woman was now seated in the posture of one writing. A strange dim light was around her, but whence it proceeded I never thought of inquiring. As if I, too, had stepped over the bourne, and was a ghost myself, all fear was now gone. I got out of bed, and softly crossed the room to where she was seated. 'If she should be beautiful!' I thought,—for I had often dreamed of a beautiful ghost that made love to me. The figure did not move. She was looking at a faded brown paper. 'Some old love-letter,' I thought, and stepped nearer. So cool was I now, that I actually peeped over her shoulder. With mingled surprise and dismay I found that the dim page over which she bent was that of an old account-book. Ancient household records, in rusty ink, held up to the glimpses of the waning moon, which shone through the parting in the curtains, their entries of shillings and pence!—Of pounds there was not one. No doubt pounds and farthings are much the same in the world of thought,—the true spirit-world; but in the ghost-world this eagerness over shillings and pence must mean something awful! To think that coins which had since been worn smooth in other pockets and purses, which had gone back to the Mint, and been melted down, to come out again and yet again with the heads of new kings and queens,—that dinners, eaten by men and women and children whose bodies had since been eaten by the worms,—that polish for the floors, inches of whose thickness had since been worn away,—that the hundred nameless trifles of a life utterly vanished, should be perplexing, annoying, and worst of all, interesting the soul of a ghost who had been in Hades for centuries! The writing was very old-fashioned, and the words were con-tracted. I could read nothing but the moneys and one single entry,—' Corinths, Vs.'

" Currants for a Christmas pudding, most likely! —Ah, poor lady! the pudding and not the Christ-mas was her care; not the delight of the children over it, but the beggarly pence which it cost. And she cannot get it out of her head, although her brain was ' powdered all as thin as flour ' ages ago in the mortar of Death. ' Alas, poor ghost!'　It needs no treasured hoard left behind, no floor stained with the blood of the murdered child, no wickedly hidden parchment of landed rights!—An old account-book is enough for the hell of the house-keeping gentlewoman!

"She never lifted her face, or seemed to know that I stood behind her.　I left her, and went into the bow window, where I could see her face. I was right.　It was the same old lady I had met in Russell Square, walking in front of James Hetheridge.　Her withered lips went moving as if they would have uttered words had the breath been commissioned thither; her brow was con- tracted over her thin nose; and once and again her shining forefinger went up to her temple as if she were pondering some deep problem of humanity.　How long I stood gazing at her I do not know, but at last I withdrew to my bed, and left her struggling to solve that which she could never solve thus. It was the symbolic problem of her own life, and she had failed to read it. I remember nothing more. She may be sitting there still, solving at the insolvable.

"I should have felt no inclination, with the broad sun of the squire's face, the keen eyes of James, and the beauty of Lætitia before me at the breakfast-table, to say a word about what I had seen, even if I had not been afraid of the doubt concerning my sanity which the story would certainly awaken. What with the memories of the night and the want of my spectacles, I passed a very dreary day, dreading the return of the night, for, cool as I had been in her presence, I could not regard the possible reappearance of the ghost with equanimity. But when the night did come, I slept soundly till the morning.

"The next day, not being able to read with comfort, I went wandering about the place, and at length began to fit the outside and inside of the house together. It was a large and rambling edifice, parts of it very old, parts comparatively modern. I first found my own window, which looked out of the back. Below this window, on one side, there was a door. I wondered whither it led, but found it locked. At the moment James approached from the stables. 'Where does this door lead?' I asked him. 'I will get the key,' he answered. 'It is rather a queer old place. We used to like it when we were children.' 'There's a stair, you see,' he said, as he threw the door open. 'It leads up over the kitchen.' I followed him up the stair. 'There's a door into your room,' he said, 'but it's always locked now.—And here's Grannie's room, as they call it, though why, I have not the least idea,' he added, as he pushed open the door of an old-fashioned parlour, smelling very musty. A few old books lay on a side-table. A china bowl stood beside them, with some shrivelled, scentless rose-leaves in the bottom of it. The cloth that covered the table was riddled by moths, and the spider-legged chairs were covered with dust.

"A conviction seized me that the old bureau must have belonged to this room, and I soon found the place where I judged it must have stood. But the same moment I caught sight of a portrait on the wall above the spot I had fixed upon. 'By Jove!' I cried, involuntarily, 'that's the very old lady I met in Russell Square!'

"'Nonsense!' said James. 'Old-fashioned ladies are like babies,—they all look the same. That's a very old portrait.'

"'So I see,' I answered. 'It is like a Zucchero.

"'I don't know whose it is,' he answered hurriedly, and I thought he looked a little queer.

" 'Is she one of the family?' I asked.

" 'They say so; but who or what she was, I don't know. You must ask Letty,' he answered.

" 'The more I look at it,' I said, 'the more I am convinced it is the same old lady.'

" 'Well,' he returned with a laugh, 'my old nurse used to say she was rather restless. But it's all nonsense.'

" 'That bureau in my room looks about the same date as this furniture,' I remarked.

" 'It used to stand just there,' he answered, pointing to the space under the picture. 'Well I remember with what awe we used to regard it; for they said the old lady kept her accounts at it still. We never dared touch the bundles of yellow papers in the pigeon-holes. I remember thinking Letty a very heroine once when she touched one of them with the tip of her forefinger. She had got yet more courageous by the time she had it moved into her own room.'

"'Then that is your sister's room I am occupying?' I said.

"'Yes.'

"'I am ashamed of keeping her out of it.'

"'Oh! she'll do well enough.'

"'If I were she though,' I added, 'I would send that bureau back to its own place.'

"'What do you mean, Heywood? Do you believe every old wife's tale that ever was told?'

"'She may get a fright some day,—that's all!' I replied.

"He smiled with such an evident mixture of pity and contempt that for the moment I almost disliked him; and feeling certain that Lætitia would receive any such hint in a somewhat similar manner, I did not feel inclined to offer her any advice with regard to the bureau.

"Little occurred during the rest of my visit worthy of remark. Somehow or other I did not make much progress with Lætitia. I believe I had begun to see into her character a little, and therefore did not get deeper in love as the days went on. I know I became less absorbed in her society, although I was still anxious to make myself agreeable to her,—or perhaps, more properly, to give her a favourable impression of me. I do not know whether she perceived any difference in my behaviour, but I remember that I began again to remark the pinched look of her nose, and to be a little annoyed with her for always putting aside my book. At the same time, I daresay I was provoking, for I never was given to tidiness myself.

"At length Christmas-Day arrived. After breakfast, the squire, James, and the two girls arranged to walk to church. Lætitia was not in the room at the moment. I excused myself on the ground of a headache, for I had had a bad night. When they left, I went up to my room, threw myself on the bed, and was soon fast asleep.

"How long I slept I do not know, but I woke again with that indescribable yet well-known sense of not being alone. The feeling was scarcely less terrible in the daylight than it had been in the darkness. With the same sudden effort as before, I sat up in the bed. There was the figure at the open bureau, in precisely the same position as on the former occasion. But I could not see it so distinctly. I rose as gently as I could, and approached it, after the first physical terror. I am not a coward. Just as I got near enough to see the account-book open on the folding cover of the bureau, she started up, and, turning, revealed the face of Lætitia. She blushed crimson.

"'I beg your pardon, Mr. Heywood,' she said, in great confusion ; 'I thought you had gone to church with the rest.'

"'I had lain down with a headache, and gone to sleep,' I replied. 'But,—forgive me, Miss Hetheridge,' I added, for my mind was full of the dreadful coincidence,—'don't you think you would have been better at church than balancing your accounts on Christmas-Day?'

"'The better day the better deed,' she said, with a somewhat offended air, and turned to walk from the room.

"'Excuse me, Lætitia,' I resumed, very seriously, 'but I want to tell you something.'

"She looked conscious. It never crossed me, that perhaps she fancied I was going to make a confession. Far other things were then in my mind. For I thought how awful it was, if she too, like the ancestral ghost, should have .

to do an age-long penance of haunting that bureau and those horrid figures, and I had suddenly resolved to tell her the whole story. She listened with varying complexion and face half turned aside. When I had ended, which I fear I did with something of a personal appeal, she lifted her head and looked me in the face, with just a slight curl on her thin lip, and answered me. 'If I had wanted a sermon, Mr. Heywood, I should have gone to church for it. As for the ghost, I am sorry for you.' So saying she walked out of the room.

"The rest of the day I did not find very merry. I pleaded my headache as an excuse for going to bed early. How I hated the room now! Next morning, immediately after breakfast, I took my leave of Lewton Grange."

"And lost a good wife, perhaps, for the sake of a ghost, uncle!" said Janet.

"If I lost a wife at all, it was a stingy one. I should have been ashamed of her all my life long."

"Better than a spendthrift," said Janet.

"How do you know that?" returned her uncle. "All the difference I see is, that the extravagant ruins the rich, and the stingy robs the poor."

"But perhaps she repented, uncle," said Kate.

"I don't think she did, Katey. Look here."

Uncle Cornelius drew from the breast-pocket of his coat a black-edged letter.

"I have kept up my friendship with her brother," he said. "All he knows about the matter is, that either we had a quarrel, or she refused me;—he is not sure which. I must say for Lætitia, that she was no tattler. Well, here's a letter I had from James this very morning. I will read it to you.

"'My dear Heywood,—We have had a terrible shock this morning. Letty did not come down to breakfast, and Lizzie went to see if she was ill. We heard her scream, and, rushing up, there was poor Letty, sitting at the old bureau, quite dead. She had fallen forward on the desk, and her housekeeping-book was crumpled up under her. She had been so all night long, we suppose, for she was not undressed, and was quite cold. The doctors say it was disease of the heart.'

"There !" said Uncle Cornie, folding up the letter.

"Do you think the ghost had anything to do with it, uncle?" asked Kate, almost under her breath.

"How should I know, my dear? Possibly."

"It's very sad," said Janet; "but I don't see the good of it all. If the ghost had come to tell that she had hidden away money in some secret place in the old bureau, one would see why she had been permitted to come back. But what was the good of those accounts after they were over and done with? I don't believe in the ghost."

"Ah, Janet, Janet! but those wretched accounts were not over and done with, you see. That is the misery of it."

Uncle Cornelius rose without another word, bade them good night, and walked out into the wind.

THE END.

Butler & Tanner, The Selwood Printing Works, Frome, and London.